THEY RODE TO EL PASO

Branson Howard—A captain of the Texas Rangers, he worked hard to put a violent past behind him and use his gun-skills to uphold law and order in a place teeming with trouble.

Turk Killam—Behind the legitimate front of a profitable ranch, he organized a criminal operation that would make him undisputed master of the range and bring ruin upon El Paso.

Jack Taubert—Ex-con, outlaw, and freelance double-crosser, his avowed goal was to die rich—and to take down whoever stood in his way.

Lucy Daniels—Killam's beautiful stepdaughter, she possessed courage and brains enough to stand up against what she knew was wrong, knowing the high price she must pay in doing it.

The Stagecoach Series
Ask your bookseller for the books you have missed

STAGECOACH STATION 23:
EL PASO

Hank Mitchum

™

Created by the producers of
White Indian, Children of the
Lion, Stagecoach, and Saga of the
Southwest.

Chairman of the Board: Lyle Kenyon Engel

BANTAM BOOKS

TORONTO • NEW YORK • LONDON • SYDNEY • AUCKLAND

STAGECOACH STATION 23: EL PASO

*A Bantam Book / published by arrangement with
Book Creations, Inc.*

Bantam edition / April 1986

*Produced by Book Creations, Inc.
Chairman of the Board: Lyle Kenyon Engel*

ISBN 0-553-25549-5

Published simultaneously in the United States and Canada

PRINTED IN THE UNITED STATES OF AMERICA

H   0 9 8 7 6 5 4 3 2 1

STAGECOACH STATION 23:
EL PASO

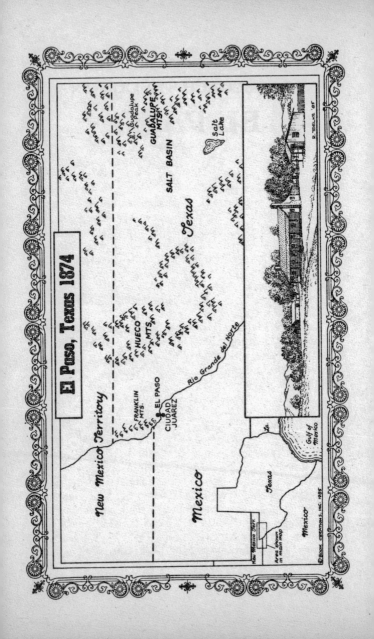

El Paso, Texas 1874

New Mexico Territory

Franklin MTS.

HUECO MTS.

EL PASO

CIUDAD JUAREZ

Rio Grande del Norte

GUADALUPE MTS.

Guadalupe Peak

SALT BASIN

Salt Lake

Texas

Mexico

R. TOELLE '85

New Mexico Terr.

Area shown in main map

Texas

Mexico

Gulf of Mexico

©BOOK CREATIONS, INC. 1985

Chapter One

The lone rider pulled his bay gelding to a halt in the brutal heat, slitting his eyes against the biting glare reflected off the white landscape. Dismounting, he winced as his boots touched the burning salt desert. He lifted his broad-brimmed Stetson and sleeved away the sweat from his brow. The blazing single eye of the midday sun licked his face with fire. Turning away, he lifted the canvas-covered canteen from the saddle horn and felt the sun burn like red-hot needles into his sweat-stained back.

Carefully, Captain Branson Howard of the Texas Rangers poured a ration of the precious liquid into his hat and let the bay drink. He then allowed himself a half-dozen swallows from the canteen. Capping it, he looped the leather strap over the saddle horn.

Shielding his dry, red-rimmed eyes with his hat, the Ranger gazed northward. There stood Guadalupe Peak, lifting its jagged, majestic head some 8,750 feet toward the sky. He had first spotted the peak two days ago; it had taken him that long to draw abreast of it.

It was August 18, 1874, and Branson Howard was sixteen days out of Austin, headquarters for the Texas Rangers. He had come five hundred miles in that time, averaging just over thirty miles a day. He was now in the middle of the great salt basin in west Texas, just south of the New Mexico border.

Patting the horse's sweaty neck, the Ranger said, "Sorry we can't ride when it's cool at night, but I can't risk having you stumble in the dark and break a leg.

1

But just three more days, Buck, and we'll be in El Paso. Then you can drink all the water you can hold and get yourself a well-deserved rest." The bay bobbed his head and nickered, as if he understood his master's words.

Branson stepped into the stirrup and eased himself slowly onto the blistering saddle. He nudged the big animal westward and narrowed his eyes against the painful glare. As he moved slowly in the direction of El Paso, Branson studied the burning salt flats through the dancing heat waves. It was an endless arid wasteland where water was almost as scarce as human habitation. There was absolutely no vegetation and no sign of animal life. In some primeval day, this basin had been a great body of water, lapping its waves against salty shores in every direction. But in August of 1874, moisture to this dry, cracked white land seemed only an ancient memory.

The Texas Ranger finished his day as the western horizon swallowed the sun. He fed the bay from the sack of oats that rode behind the saddle; then he watered him. He gave the animal a brisk rubdown as twilight stole away the orange of the sunset, then tended to his own needs.

After a supper of beef jerky, hardtack, beans, and water, Branson stretched out on the saddle blanket and pillowed his head on the saddle. A slight breeze came up, cooling his tortured body. He wished for a good bath, but that would have to wait. He could not spare water from his two canteens even to wash his dust-caked face. Man and animal would need every drop to moisten their throats for the next three days.

To take full advantage of the cool breeze, the Ranger sat up and peeled off his shirt. Settling back on the blanket, he welcomed the goosebumps that surfaced on his skin, responding to the change in temperature.

Slowly stars appeared overhead. Branson Howard's thoughts strayed back over the twenty-nine years of his life. Childhood memories flitted through his mind, rushing by quickly and then stopping suddenly on the blackest day in his life. . . .

The streets of Laredo were busy that Saturday afternoon. It was May 3, 1863, Branson Howard's eighteenth birthday. He had driven with his father, Lloyd, and his mother, Sadie, into town from their small ranch to stock up on supplies. But more important, Branson was going to get a new pair of high-heeled Texas boots for his birthday.

Pulling the wagon to a halt in front of Becker's General Store, Lloyd said, "Sadie, you go on in and tell Bob what you need. The boy and I will walk over to Fanning's and get his boots. We'll be back before you're done."

Twenty minutes later, the lanky youth clomped across Laredo's dusty main street alongside his father in his new high-heeled boots.

Lloyd Howard laughed. "Those heels put you over six feet tall, son. If you ever get any meat on those bones of yours, you'll be a good-sized man."

Branson was about to comment on his father's words, when the thunder of hooves filled his ears. He looked up to see four riders galloping abreast down the street, bearing down on them.

Suddenly Lloyd shouted, "Look out, son!" and attempted to push him out of the way. One of the horses brushed the youth, knocking him down. As he rolled in the dust, he heard his father curse at the careless riders. They drew up suddenly and wheeled their mounts.

Lloyd rushed to Branson with concern in his eyes. Helping him up, he asked, "Are you hurt, boy?"

"I'm all right, Pa," responded the youth, brushing himself off.

Abruptly, a cold voice pierced the warm spring air. "Hey, mister! Did I hear you right?"

Father and son turned to face the four riders. The one second from their left had spoken; it was his horse that had knocked Branson down.

"You heard me exactly right!" blustered the elder

Howard. "Stupid fools charging through town like that.
You could have killed my boy!"

Mottled patches of red flushed the rider's cheeks.
Fixing Lloyd with a hard look, he said, "I don't think
you know who you're talkin' to, mister!"

Lloyd Howard's temper was hot. "A jackass is a jackass!" he snapped. "His name makes no difference."

The man's expression turned as hard and rough as
rimrock. "*You're talkin' to Tate Raley, mister,*" he hissed
through his teeth.

Branson Howard felt a cold shiver run up his spine.
Tate Raley was well known in these parts. He was a
cold-blooded killer and lightning fast with his gun. Touching his father on the shoulder, he said, "It's okay, Pa.
I'm not hurt. Just forget it. Let these men go on about
their business."

"Too late for that, sonny," came Raley's voice like
cold wind across an icy lake. Throwing his leg over the
saddle and touching ground, he added, "Your old man
has a big mouth. He's gonna draw against me, now."

"Pa . . ." came Branson's tremulous voice.

Squaring his shoulders, Lloyd Howard said, "Go in
the store with your ma, boy."

"But Pa," argued the youth, "this man is a gunfighter. You're *not*. You don't stand a ch—"

"You're pa's wearin' a gun, kid!" cut in Raley. "A man
shouldn't wear one unless he knows how to pull it and
use it."

Lloyd Howard turned his back toward the store,
repeating his command for Branson to go inside. People
on the street began to scatter as Tate Raley took his
stance. The gunman would not allow the rancher to get
set. His hand shot downward. Branson leaped from the
line of fire.

Sadie Howard had heard the harsh voices from inside
the store. At the same instant Raley's gun was coming
out of its holster, she appeared in the doorway, shriek-
ing her husband's name.

Lloyd had started his draw. Sadie's cry pulled his
head around as Raley's gun roared. Lloyd buckled,

swinging his gun upward. Raley fanned his weapon repeatedly in response. It spit fire rapidly. Bullets struck Lloyd three times and Sadie twice.

Stunned, Branson Howard watched both his parents die under Tate Raley's gun. While he ran to them, Raley mounted his horse and galloped away with his friends.

Sweat beaded the Texas Ranger's brow as he momentarily returned to the present. He sleeved away the moisture and allowed his mind to slip into the past once again. Forcing his thoughts away from the painful ordeal of the double funeral, he focused on the vengeance that had burned in his heart when he entered Bill Foss's gun shop and bought a used Navy Colt .44 and a worn, well-oiled holster.

Joe Medford, Laredo's town marshal, showed up at the ranch a few days later. Young Branson was practicing the fast draw when Medford rode in and dismounted.

"I heard in town that you bought that gun, kid," said the marshal, walking toward him.

Branson Howard's sharp hazel eyes fixed Medford with a cold stare. "So?"

"Word is that you're practicing up so's you can go after Tate Raley."

"You've got it right," said the youth evenly.

"Better let the law handle it, son."

Branson looked at the marshal as if he had just seen him for the first time. "Let the law handle it?" he mocked. "It was a week ago today that Raley murdered my parents. What's the law doing about it? Has Raley been arrested? No! He's still on the loose so he can murder somebody else!"

"These things take time, Branson," said Medford placatingly. "Just give us a little time. We'll get him."

Branson Howard's vengeful eyes looked the lawman up and down. "You're mighty patient about it."

"That's part of the procedure, son."

"I'll tell you why you're so patient, Marshal," said Branson, a contemptuous anger staining his words. "It wasn't *your* parents Tate Raley gunned down."

"I realize that, son, but—"

"While you're idly playing with *procedure*, sir," breathed the youth, clipping the words between his teeth, "I'm going to master the fast draw. I'll get to where I'm faster than Raley. If your *procedure* hasn't put him at the end of a rope by that time, you can forget it. I'll track him down, and he'll face me . . . and die!"

"The man has been slapping leather for five or six years, kid," countered Medford. "You can't match his draw in a few weeks or even a few months."

"I don't intend to match it, Marshal," Branson said curtly. "I intend to *beat* it."

Back on the salt flats, the Texas Ranger became aware of a meteor streaking across the night sky, followed by its long white tail. He adjusted his head on the saddle and then let his thoughts return to the day he rode into Laredo for more bullets.

Upon entering Bill Foss's gun shop, Branson met the gunsmith's smile with his own.

"Hello, kid," said Foss. "The gun working okay?"

"Just fine, Mr. Foss," responded the youth. "I need some more ammunition."

Moving toward the well-stocked shelves, Foss asked, "How much, kid?"

"I'll take a case," Branson said flatly.

The words pulled Foss's head around. "A *case*?"

"Yes, sir."

"A case is six-dozen boxes, son. Are you sure you want that many? I mean, at a dollar a box, a case of .44s will cost you seventy-two dollars."

Peeling off several bills from a roll in his pocket, Branson replied, "I'm aware of the price, Mr. Foss."

The gunsmith hunched his shoulders, saying he would get a case from the storeroom in the back. Returning and setting the heavy box on the counter, he cleared his throat and said, "Branson, word is all over town that you are going to track down Tate Raley and challenge him."

"So?"

"None of us want to see you get killed, son," said Foss with concern in his eyes. "Why don't you just let the law deal with Raley?"

Fixing his hazel eyes on the older man, Branson said, "How long, now, since my ma and pa were gunned down, Mr. Foss?"

The gunsmith rubbed his chin. "Well, let's see . . . must be about six weeks, now."

"Seven, to be exact," the youth said tonelessly. "Has Tate Raley been brought to justice?"

"Well, not yet, kid, but—"

"Sounds to me like the law isn't too eager to deal with Raley, Mr. Foss. Well, take it from me. *I am.*"

"But, Branson, Tate Raley is a seasoned gunfighter," argued Foss. "You've never even pulled a gun against another man before, much less killed one."

"Raley had his first time, didn't he?" parried Branson.

"Well, yes, but—"

"He will also have his last," added Branson with sand in his voice. "I aim to be the last man he ever draws on."

Branson Howard lay under the shimmering canopy of stars and thought of how he had practiced drawing and firing six hours every day for another two weeks. Each day he marked progress in both speed and accuracy. He seemed to have a natural knack for handling the weapon. He had no way to compare his quickness of draw against that of the man he intended to challenge. The only thing he could do was practice until his instincts told him he was ready. He figured to hone himself another two months. Then he would go after his parents' killer. When he was low on ammunition again, he rode into town to buy some more.

It was midmorning when Branson entered Laredo and dismounted in front of the gun shop. The Navy .44 was slung low on his hip and thonged to his slender thigh. When his foot touched the wooden sidewalk, a familiar voice called his name from directly across the street.

The youth wheeled around to see Tate Raley leaning

against the hitch rail, flanked by his three friends. A cigarette was dangling from the corner of the gunfighter's mouth. The sight of Raley brought a flood of memories of his dead parents. The urge to kill Raley surged like fresh fire through his veins. He had wanted more practice, but it was evident by the look on Tate's face that Branson was going to have to face him now.

Raley's cold eyes bore steadily into Branson. "They tell me you're wantin' to look me up, kid," he said levelly.

Branson wondered if Marshal Medford would interfere. His eyes flicked down the street toward the lawman's office.

Tate Raley chuckled humorlessly. "Marshal ain't gonna help you, kid. He's outta town." Drawing his lungs full of smoke, he flipped the cigarette into the street and pulled away from the rail. "Folks are sayin' you've been practicin' up to challenge me for killin' your old man and your old lady."

If ever anyone was eager for revenge, it was young Branson Howard. It was evident in the hard lines of his face and in the tightwire flexing of his muscles. "Folks are telling it right," he breathed hotly, allowing no fear to overtake his thoughts.

Raley took his stance and sniffed contemptuously. "Well, hop to it," he declared as his hand snaked toward his gun.

Totally unaware of the crowd that was gathering, Branson whipped out his gun and fired. In the same split second, Raley's gun cleared leather and roared. Raley's bullet chewed into the street. There was a wild look of disbelief in his eyes as he peered at the youth through the blue-white smoke. His knees buckled, and the gun slipped from his numb fingers. He took one faltering step and then fell flat on his face. Branson's slug had entered his heart.

The crowd was instantly like a beehive. Branson Howard had outdrawn and killed Tate Raley!

As the Texas Ranger lay on the salty ground looking at the inky sky, more memories flashed through his mind. He thought of the parade of gunfighters that had come to Laredo looking for the man who had out-gunned the famous Tate Raley. By the time he turned twenty, Branson Howard had faced and killed half a dozen men.

Finally, in an effort to shed his image as a gunfighter, he had sold the ranch and left Laredo. He traveled northward across Texas, working as a ranch hand and breaking horses. But his reputation followed him. By the time he was twenty-three, Branson had killed thirteen men.

Then one day in Austin, he heard that the Texas Rangers were signing up new recruits. Suddenly, Branson Howard had his ticket to freedom. The Rangers were held in awe by decent citizens and outlaws alike. With a badge on his chest, the challenges would end.

In the six years he had been a Ranger, Branson had been forced to kill a few men, but only while attempt-ing to bring them to justice—never as part of a quick-draw challenge. Because of his alert mind and exceptional intelligence, he had moved up rapidly in the ranks of the proficient law-enforcement agency. Few men had made captain so quickly.

As the cool breeze kissed his face, Branson Howard thought of his present high-risk mission. Ranger officials in Austin had sent him to El Paso to transport a sixty-thousand-dollar gold shipment back to Austin. The gold nuggets had been mined in the mountains of New Mexico and were payment to the Republic of Texas for water rights along the Texas–New Mexico border west of El Paso.

Ranger officials had commissioned Branson to use his guts and ingenuity to get the gold safely to Austin. The last such shipment had been made by wagon with a military escort; but the many outlaws in the area had banded together until they outnumbered the troops five to one. They had ambushed the wagon train, leav-ing the soldiers dead and taking the gold.

Branson Howard had devised a plan to move the gold right past the outlaws by hauling it in an innocent-looking stagecoach. Substantial protection payments by stagecoach officials generally assured the safety of the runs, and when a robbery did occur, the passengers were unmolested, with the strongbox being the sole object of attention. Therefore, Branson planned to transport the gold in ordinary luggage. He would ride into El Paso, posing as a businessman from Las Cruces, New Mexico, and ride the stage from the border city to Austin.

Cooled off sufficiently, he sat up, pulled on his shirt, and lay back down. While thinking through the details of his plan, he fell asleep. It seemed he had been asleep only a few moments when the sound of a boot on sand snapped him awake. Opening his eyes, he saw the rotund form of a man standing over him, silhouetted against the gray dawn of the sky. Branson's hand went to his gun.

"Ah, no, gringo," said the man. "Do not touch the gun."

Checking the swing of his hand, Branson sat up, blinking to clear his vision. A dozen Mexicans, dressed in wrinkled, sand-colored uniforms stood around him, their rifles trained on his back and chest. He recognized them as Federales.

The corpulent leader who stood over him said, "We wish you no harm, señor. I am Captain Ramón Gonzales of the Mexican police. We only wish to question you."

Branson rose slowly to his feet. Stifling a yawn, he asked, "What do you want to know?"

The Mexican officer smiled, his teeth looking extra white against the black mustache and swarthy skin. "What is your name, señor?"

"I am Captain Branson Howard of the Texas Rangers."

Gonzales's heavy eyebrows arched. "The Texas Rangers? I see no badge."

"It's in my saddlebag," said Branson, feeling a touch of irritation. "What is this all about?"

"We are on the trail of three criminals who have fled from Mexico," answered the fat man, adjusting the leather strap that crossed diagonally from his shoulder to his gun belt. "We saw your horse first and then yourself asleep on the ground. We decided to inquire if you have seen the three horsemen."

"I could talk better if those guns were pointed in another direction," Branson said, sweeping a partial circle with his hand.

"Oh, of course, señor," said Gonzales, motioning for his men to lower their rifles. Swinging his gaze back to the Ranger, he waited for him to speak.

Blandly, Branson said, "I have not seen them, Captain. You and your men are the first people I have seen for nearly a week. Are these criminals Mexicans or Americans?"

There was disbelief in Gonzales's dark eyes. "They are gringos, like yourself," he answered stiffly, looking hard at Branson. "They tried to rob a bank in Guadalupe but were run off. They split up, with two men going northeast and the third coming this way to the north. We lost the trail of the other two and doubled back to try to find the loner. And now I am wondering if he might be you. I am wondering if you are really a Texas Ranger."

Branson Howard bristled. "I'll prove it to you right now," he said crustily, heading toward his horse. Suddenly, a dozen guns were leveled at him, and he halted in his tracks.

"One moment, señor," said Gonzales. "We will take a look in the saddlebags. If you speak the truth, we will be on our way. If you lie, you will rot in a Mexican prison."

Gonzales stepped up to Branson's bay gelding and poked his fingers around in the saddlebags. After a few seconds, he produced the Texas Ranger badge.

Smiling wickedly, the swarthy captain tossed the badge in the air and then caught it. Stepping close to the taller man, he said, "Now how do we know that this is *your* badge, señor? Maybe you steal it, no?"

Sudden anger colored Branson's words. "I did not steal it, Captain. It is *my* badge. I told you who I am;

now please put the badge back and be on your way. You are out of your jurisdiction."

Gonzales laughed. "The gringo has a bad temper. Does his temper show because Captain Ramón Gonzales sees through his lies?"

Branson squared his jaw. His voice was thick as he growled, "I am not lying. Dig a little deeper, and you will find my identification papers in a small leather folder."

The portly Mexican returned to the bay gelding, fumbled momentarily in the same saddlebag where he had found the badge, and closed his fingers on the leather folder. Opening it as he walked back to Branson, he read the Ranger's description carefully. "Five feet eleven inches tall," he said, eyeing him up and down. "I would say you are over six feet."

"I'm wearing boots with two-inch heels," Branson responded flatly.

Gonzales smiled. "So you are." Looking back into the folder, he said, "One hundred ninety pounds." Reading further, he eyed the Ranger again. "Hazel eyes. Dark wavy hair. This matches, but it says nothing of the mustache you are now wearing."

Perturbed, the muscular, broad-shouldered man put his hands on his hips and said, "I grew the mustache since the description was written up. Now are you satisfied?"

The Mexican studied him for a long moment and then smiled broadly. "Sí, señor, I am satisfied you are telling the truth." Extending the badge and folder to the Ranger, he said, "My apologies."

Branson nodded, accepted the items, and stuffed them back in his saddlebag.

"One of the men we are looking for is about your size, señor," Gonzales said. "Only he is totally bald. Another is very tall and quite thin. His left ear is missing. The third was stocky and wore his gun low—a gunfighter. They are killers. If you see them, it is your duty as a lawman to apprehend them and notify the Mexican government."

Branson nodded without comment. The Mexican walked to his horse, as Branson stood under the watchful gaze of the dark-faced Federales.

Easing his bulk onto the horse's back, Gonzales saluted Branson and said, *"Adiós, Señor Texas Ranger."* With that, he wheeled his horse and led his men northward in a cloud of white dust.

Chapter Two

Branson Howard continued his westward trek. On the morning of the second day, he rode out of the barren salt flats, welcoming the sight of patches of blue prickly poppy, golden rattleweed, and squat, yellow-flowered cacti. Little desert animals flitted about.

It was early afternoon when Branson topped a gentle rise and spied a patch of green in the distance, surrounded by bushes and trees. Peering through the shimmering heat waves, he studied the scene as his horse carried him closer. "Sure enough, old boy," he said finally. "It's the real thing. I was afraid it was a mirage."

Lifting his hat and sleeving away sweat, he coaxed the horse, "C'mon, boy. A little faster. Let's get us both a good drink and some cool shade!"

Outlaws Herb Nolan and Lefty Muldane stood beside the bubbling stream in the shade of the cottonwood trees. Muldane was pulling on his horse's reins, trying to force the animal toward the water. The horse stood swaying on unsteady legs, head hanging low, eyes drooped.

"It ain't no use, Lefty," said the bald-headed man. "That old nag has had it. He's gonna die on you."

"We pushed him too hard getting here," remarked the tall, skinny man.

"You wanna end up in a stinkin' Mexican jail?" chided Nolan.

"Course not. But—"

14

"We'd have never outrun those Federales if we hadn't rode hard, Lefty. You know that."

"Yeah, but your horse is younger'n mine. We could've taken it a little easier and still got away."

Herb Nolan's face hardened. "Are you forgettin' that this is the very day we're supposed to meet Vic right here on this spot?"

"Well, he ain't here yet, is he?" snapped Muldane, still tugging the sick horse in the direction of the stream.

"He'll be here," Nolan said with confidence. "It's a good thing we rode hard. Vic has plans to hold up a Tucson bank, and I sure don't want Vic upset."

"He's gonna be upset anyhow, Herb," said Muldane, letting the reins go slack. "This horse is gonna die, and we'll have to ride double on your horse to El Paso. Vic ain't gonna like being slowed up."

Before the bald man could comment, the sick horse keeled over, hitting the ground hard. He lay there, sides pumping, nostrils flared, eyes rolled back. Muldane swore, drawing his revolver.

"Hey, stupid!" spoke up Nolan. "Pull the saddle off him before you shoot him. It's easier when he's alive than workin' against dead weight."

Lefty Muldane was already quite upset over his horse. Herb's use of the word *stupid* brought a rush of blood to the skinny man's face. Whipping his gun around, he eared back the hammer and drew a bead on Nolan's face, holding the weapon in both hands. "Who's stupid?" he bellowed, eyes bulging. A muscle in his jaw was twitching.

Herb Nolan's features turned the color of dead ashes. Lifting shaky palms toward his angry partner, he said, "N-now Lefty, I d-didn't mean nothin'. I was just tryin' to save you some effort gettin' that saddle off when that critter is dead."

Muldane held the muzzle steady. Through gritted yellow teeth, he said, "I ain't stupid, Herb."

Nolan watched the black muzzle nervously, and the wild eyes behind it.

"Did you hear me, Herb?" demanded the skinny outlaw. "I ain't stupid!"

"Okay, okay," gasped Nolan. "Now put the gun down."

"Say I ain't stupid, Herb!" screeched Muldane, shaking with fury.

"Okay, Lefty," choked the bald man, "you ain't stupid!"

"Say it again, Herb!" The threatening muzzle looked like it was ready to explode.

"You ain't stupid, you ain't stupid, you ain't stupid!" screamed Nolan. "There! You satisfied?"

The skinny man's tight features relaxed. He lowered the gun, letting the hammer down slowly. "Don't you ever call me stupid again, Herb," he breathed.

Suddenly, like a panther, Herb Nolan leaped at Muldane, seized the revolver, and threw it in the stream. Lefty was taken by surprise. Before he could react, Nolan slammed him solidly on the jaw with a rock-hard fist. The skinny man went down, and Nolan pounced on him, pummeling him with both fists. As Muldane fought back, Nolan gripped a wrist, rolled Muldane over, and rammed the arm unmercifully up behind his head. Muldane howled, cursing his assailant violently, but Nolan merely shoved the arm upward, inflicting more pain.

Breathing hotly, Nolan said, "Don't you ever throw a gun on me again, Lefty! You hear me? I'll tear your arm off and beat you over the head with it! You hear me?"

Wincing in agony, Muldane ejected a painful, "Yes."

Shoving harder, Nolan said, "Say it, Lefty."

"Say what?" squeaked the skinny outlaw.

"Say you'll never throw a gun on me again!"

Sucking in air through clenched teeth, Muldane complied. "I'll never throw a gun on you again!"

With that, Nolan released him and let him up. Muldane got to his feet, rubbing his arm and shoulder, giving his partner a sour look. "You didn't have to toss my gun in the water," he mumbled.

While Muldane headed toward the stream to retrieve his revolver, Herb Nolan's attention was drawn to something that was moving among the heat waves on the desert, due east. "Hold it, Lefty!" he called. "Look over there."

Muldane halted at the water's edge, looked over his shoulder at the bald man, and then followed the direction of his finger. His eyes focused on the lone rider coming toward them.

"Hey, it's Vic!" shouted Lefty.

"It ain't Vic," Herb said evenly.

"But we sure enough have got company comin'."

Lefty Muldane stared at the approaching horse and rider for a long moment. Without turning around to look at his partner, he said, "Hey, Herb, are you thinking what I'm thinking?"

Nolan chuckled deep in his chest. "Looks like you got yourself a new horse, Lefty."

The skinny man danced with glee on the bank of the stream. Starting into the water, he said, "I'll get my gun."

"Let it go for now," said Nolan. "Just get the rifle from your saddle and let's plan this thing out. That rider will be here in a few minutes."

Muldane leaned over his dying horse and slipped the rifle from the boot. The animal's sides were still heaving, its breath dry and reedy.

"Now, here's what we'll do," said Nolan as Muldane came over to him. "We'll be friendly as he rides in. If he suspects anythin' right off, he could make a run for it, and we'd lose that horse."

"Sure don't want to do that," commented Muldane, his eyes flashing with excitement.

"We'll wait till he dismounts," continued Nolan. "As soon as his right foot touches the ground, I'll draw on him. Then you put that rifle on him, too. When I see the time is right to kill him, I'll shoot. You get him with the rifle, too. Got it?"

Lefty Muldane grinned and nodded.

"Lean the rifle here in this creosote bush," Nolan said, touching Muldane's bony shoulder. "You get it when I pull my revolver and cock it. Just act like you're doin' somethin' with one of your boots. I'll pretend I'm

workin' on my cinch. Go on, sit down. He's gettin'
closer."

Branson Howard set his horse toward the tiny green
oasis that shimmered in the distant heat waves. When
they were within a half mile, the bay's ears perked up
and he began to nicker.

"You smell the water, don't you, boy?" chuckled his
master, patting his neck. The horse went into a trot,
covering the distance quickly.

Suddenly, Branson was aware of dark forms under
the trees. He studied the area through the heat waves.
He could make out a man and a horse—a blue roan. As
he drew within a hundred yards, the Ranger could see
a second horse lying on the ground, probably dead.
Then he saw another man, sitting in the dust, fiddling
with one of his boots. The men and horses were on the
far side of a small stream.

The bay broke into a gallop the last sixty yards, eager
to get to the water. Branson let him step into the
ten-foot-wide stream and sink his muzzle into its shallow depths. Remaining in the saddle, he eyed the two
men as they took a few steps in his direction and then
stopped, side by side.

"Hello," called Branson above the slurping of his
horse.

"Afternoon," nodded the shorter man.

"Howdy," returned the tall, thin one.

As the shorter one lifted his hat and mopped sweat
with a bandanna, the Ranger noticed that he was bald.
Instantly, he remembered Captain Gonzales's description of the gringo outlaws he was chasing. These two fit
perfectly; one was bald, the other was missing his left
ear.

"Looks like you've got a plumb thirsty horse there,
mister," said Nolan, wishing the man would dismount
so they could have a surefire opportunity to kill him
without hurting the horse.

"He hasn't had much water since we hit the Salt

Basin four days ago," said Branson. Flicking his gaze to
the sorrel on the ground, he noticed it was still alive.
"Looks like you've got a sick one."

"Yeah," said Muldane. "He got me this far, then just
plain gave out."

"Where'd you fellas come from?" queried Branson in
an amiable tone.

Both men answered simultaneously, Muldane saying,
"Mexico," and Nolan saying, "Pecos." Nolan gave his
partner a dirty look and said, "We were in Mexico some
time ago, but we've been across the border in Pecos for
three months. My partner never can remember nothin'."

Branson smiled and nodded. Pulling the bay's head
up, he said, "That's enough for a while, boy. We'll let
you cool down. Then you can have some more."

While nudging the animal toward the west bank,
Branson pondered the situation. Gonzales had said there
was a third man who had split up with these two during
the pursuit. Possibly this oasis was a rendezvous spot.
As a Texas Ranger, it was Branson's duty to put them
under arrest and take them into El Paso, where the
sheriff could contact the Mexican authorities. They were
probably wanted north of the border, too, Branson
guessed. He would have to find a way to get the drop
on them.

Nolan and Muldane poised themselves as the stranger
guided his horse onto the bank and drew rein. Remaining in the saddle momentarily, Branson looked down at
Muldane's dying sorrel and said, "Looks like the poor
beast will have to be put out of his misery."

"We were just talkin' about it," spoke up Nolan. "I
do think he's a goner."

"You'd be doing him a favor to get it over with,"
Branson said, swinging his right leg over the bay's back
to dismount. As he did so, he heard the familiar sound
of a hammer being cocked. Touching ground, he saw
the bald man holding his revolver on him. The skinny
one dived for his rifle and aimed it at his midsection.

Branson Howard eyed them coldly. "What's going
on?"

With a wicked sneer, Nolan said, "We're takin' your horse, mister."

Slowly squaring himself with them, Branson locked a fierce gaze on the two outlaws and spoke with the sound of flint scraping on steel. "I would advise you to think that one over, boys. I'm a Texas Ranger. You want to boil yourselves up a hot kettle of fish?"

Lefty Muldane guffawed, looking at his partner. "Hey, Herb! You hear that? This peckerwood says he's a Texas Ranger!"

While Muldane broke into a laugh, Nolan said, "Who you think you're dealin' with, mister? A couple of idiots? You ain't no Texas Ranger! If you was, you'd be wearin' a uniform!"

Branson's hands were hanging loosely at his sides. So far they had not thought to make him raise them. "How many Texas Rangers did you ever see?" he asked Nolan.

"None that I remember. Why?"

"The Rangers don't wear uniforms. We wear our own clothes."

"There ain't no badge on your chest!" Nolan spat back.

"I'm on a special assignment. Badge is in my saddlebag, if you want to check it."

Muldane swore and spit into the dust. "What difference does it make if you *are* a Texas Ranger? We need your horse, so we're gonna take it."

With an acid tone, Branson said, "If you take my horse, you are interfering with official business of the Texas government. I don't think you would like the consequences."

Muldane spit again, pointing the rifle dangerously. "If we kill you and bury your carcass out here in this desert, nobody will ever know what happened—even the almighty Texas Rangers!" Speaking to his partner, while holding his wild eyes on the Ranger, he said, "How about it, Herb? Can we do it now? Can we shoot him?"

Herb Nolan's eyes were thoughtful. "I don't know, Lefty," he said in a tone of uncertainty. "This Ranger business puts a new light on it. I don't want to have to dodge them Texas Rangers the rest of my life."

"Aw, come on, Herb," Muldane whined, looking at him from the corner of his eye. "Who's gonna know? We'll bury him deep. They'll never find him. Even if they do, they'd have no way of tying him to *us*."

Nolan's gun was held steady on the Ranger's chest. "We'd better think about Vic," he said with a cautious tone. "If we get the Rangers after us, they'll be on his tail, too."

"Ain't gonna be no Rangers after us, Herb!" snapped Muldane. "I tell you, they'll never tie it to us!"

"They have ways you don't know about!" Nolan snapped back. "Now, I say let's wait till Vic gets here."

Lefty Muldane, proud of his connection with the noted outlaw and gunfighter, asked Branson, "Hey, Ranger, you ever hear of Vic Barry?"

The name was quite familiar to Branson. Barry was a coldhearted bank robber who would kill at the drop of a hat. He was wanted from Dakota to Mexico. He was also feared for his skill with the fast draw, having faced and dropped some of the fastest guns on the frontier.

"I've heard of him," Branson blandly answered.

"Well, me and Herb are his partners. We're going on a bank robbing spree, starting in Tucson."

"Shut up!" snarled Nolan. "No sense in spillin' your guts to this Ranger!"

"Why?" Muldane laughed. "He ain't gonna tell no law about it or anybody else. We gotta kill him. If we just took his animal, it wouldn't be long before he and his Ranger buddies would be breathing down our necks. He's got to die, Herb."

Branson saw the truth of it settle into Herb Nolan's eyes. His mind flashed back to his gunfighting days. Twice before he had faced men holding a cocked revolver on him. In both cases, he had drawn his gun and killed them before they could fire. But then it had been one at a time. Now he faced two men.

Suddenly the argument stopped. Both outlaws fixed their eyes on Branson Howard, taking in his alert hazel eyes, the solid bulk of his shoulders, his slender hips, and the well-worn holster. Never dreaming he could get the gun out so fast, they began to shoot at him.

Branson's hand was a blur. Four distinct gunshots split the hot desert air. Two were the Ranger's, both finding their marks. He hit Nolan first, anticipating the revolver would fire a split second ahead of the rifle. Nolan's bullet whizzed past Branson, striking his bay gelding. The slug from Muldane's rifle plowed dirt.

As the late afternoon breeze carried away the gun smoke, both outlaws lay sprawled on the ground. The Ranger made sure they were both dead and then hurried to his horse. The bay lay on its side within inches of the dying sorrel. Nolan's slug had ripped into the bay's neck, and blood was spilling onto the sand. Branson's face lost its color.

The horse nickered softly as Branson kneeled down and stroked his long face. Misty eyed, he said, "You've got a bad one, old fella. You've been a faithful partner . . . carried me many a mile. I hope you understand. There's no way I can mend your wounds, and I can't let you lie here and slowly bleed to death. You're in a lot of pain. I . . . I have to end it. You understand, don't you?"

The wounded gelding nickered weakly.

With leaden heart, Branson Howard rose to his feet mechanically and lifted the revolver from its holster. Aiming the muzzle just behind an ear, he thumbed back the hammer. The horse nickered again, just before the shot clattered across the desert floor.

The Ranger took a step toward Lefty Muldane's dying sorrel, and another shot rang out.

Minutes later, Branson Howard tightened the cinch of his own saddle on Herb Nolan's blue roan and looped the full canteens over the saddle horn. Swinging aboard, he eyed the two dead outlaws. "I'll let your friend Vic see to your burial, boys," he said dryly. He wished he could stay and apprehend Vic Barry, but he was on special assignment and would have to wire his headquarters from El Paso and leave it for them to carry out.

He took a last look at the lifeless form of his horse and said, "Good-bye, Buck. I'm sorry it happened this way." Then he rode away.

Chapter Three

At the same moment that Ranger Branson Howard was swinging aboard the blue roan out on the desert, a slender straw-haired rider was making his way into El Paso from the east.

The town was teeming with people and bustling with excitement. There were banners strung over San Francisco Street, along with posters and placards everywhere, announcing the Rio Grande Valley Horse Races that would take place just north of town the next day.

Spotting the Broken Horseshoe Saloon, the wire-thin rider pulled up at the hitch rail and slid from the saddle. He looped the reins around the rail and ducked underneath. Just as his foot touched the boardwalk, he heard a voice call out, "Jack Taubert! Hey, Jack!"

Coming down the walk was a seedy-looking man, waving his arms. "Jack Taubert!" he exclaimed, drawing near. "You old horse thief! What are you doing in El Paso?"

A smile broke out on Jack Taubert's long, angular face as he recognized Bud Hatch. They had been prison mates at Huntsville.

The two ex-convicts shook hands. "I hardly knew you," said Hatch, cuffing Jack on a bony shoulder. "I never saw you with your hair so long. I think you're skinnier than ever, too!"

Jack Taubert's shaggy yellow hair protruded in an unkempt manner from under his black, flat-crowned, sweat-stained hat. It dangled in matted tangles and bounced on his narrow shoulders when he walked. His one hundred and forty pounds clung tightly to a scrawny five-foot-ten-inch frame. A well-used Colt .45 hung low on his hip, thonged to his thigh. He was shifty eyed, with rock-hard features prematurely marked by lines of age. At twenty-six, he looked ten years older.

The two old friends cast a wary look at the passersby around them and stepped to a quiet place between two buildings. Referring to the length of his hair in a lowered voice, Jack said, "You remember how they kept cuttin' my hair in prison? Wouldn't let me wear it like I wanted to. Well, they can't keep me from it now. How long you been out, Bud?"

"Almost a year," came the reply. "They let me out about four months after you were released." Looking Jack straight in the eye, he asked, "Did you ever hit that big bonanza you were always talking about? Are you filthy rich yet?"

The slender man's face pinched. "Not yet," he replied, "but it's coming."

"You mean you've got something good going?"

Jack dipped his chin. "Well, not exactly."

"Aw, come on, Jack," Hatch ribbed him. "All that talk while we were in Huntsville! You were gonna be a millionaire by the time you'd been out six months! I mean, you had dollar signs in your eyeballs. You ate, drank, walked, talked, breathed, and slept money. I thought you would own a whole town somewhere by now."

"Well, it hasn't worked out exactly like I planned, Bud," Jack said defensively. "It ain't my fault, though. I just had a run of bad luck."

Hatch ran his gaze toward the street where crowds of people milled about. Looking back at his friend, he said, "Look, Jack, I'm on my way to see a man on some important business. How about I go see him and meet you back at the Broken Horseshoe? It won't take me more than half an hour. I'll buy the drinks, and we can talk over old times."

A tight grin curved Jack Taubert's thin lips. "Sounds good to me."

Leaning close, Hatch spoke in a low voice. "Look, Jack, old pal. I *do* have something good going. Maybe I can get you in on it."

Jack's eyes lit up. "Yeah?"

"I'm running with a gang headed by a man named Turk Killam. Making myself a bundle of money."

Jack's face took on a new light. "Go on."

Hatch looked around to make sure that no one was within earshot. "Killam fronts his operation with a legitimate ranch west of El Paso. Does real well. He's looking for a good man to bring into the gang to replace Dexter Wilson. Dexter got killed a couple weeks ago during a stagecoach holdup just outside of Santa Fe."

"How much money you pullin' in personally?" Jack asked.

"Man, I've pocketed six thousand so far this year," replied Hatch, grinning broadly. "Nothing to sneeze at, huh?"

"Not bad," nodded his avaricious friend. "You think this Turk Killam might be interested in my talents?"

"If you're as tough as I think you are and can handle that gun on your hip like you always bragged you could, I can almost guarantee he'll hire you."

"I can handle it," said Jack, jutting his pointed chin.

"That's the spirit!" Hatch laughed, patting him on the back. "I'll meet you in the saloon in half an hour."

Jack Taubert watched his friend move out from between the buildings and dissolve into the crowd. Slowly, he made his way to the boardwalk and strolled down the street. In the next block, he found Hanson's General Store and entered.

The building was hot and stuffy. Jack told himself that all general stores looked and smelled the same. He could see only one customer in the store at the moment—a woman, plump and fifty. The proprietor was busy showing her some bolts of newly acquired fabric at the rear of the store.

The skinny outlaw stepped furtively around the counter and grabbed a box of cigarette papers and two sacks of tobacco. He was turning to leave when he noticed a young boy, some ten years of age, eyeing him with open suspicion. The lad had come around a stack of boxes and stood between Jack and the door.

"Get out of the way, kid," the outlaw said, moving toward him.

"I can holler real loud, mister," warned the boy, not moving an inch. "You'd better put that stuff back. The marshal is out there on the boardwalk. I just saw him."

Jack paused, throwing a glance toward the door. People were passing by, but he saw no lawman. "You're lying," he half whispered. "There ain't no marshal out there."

"You want I should holler?" challenged the boy.

Nervously, the yellow-haired outlaw looked over his shoulder. Hanson and the plump woman were still engaged in conversation. He took another step toward the door, and the boy drew in a breath, ready to shout. Jack stopped again. He considered lunging at his youthful challenger. He would cover his mouth, then slam him on the head with his gun barrel. However, the distance between them made such a move too risky. The boy could yell before Jack would have a chance to cover his mouth.

There was only one thing to do. He would have to replace the stolen articles. "Okay, kid," he said in resignation. "I'll put this stuff back."

As Jack turned, the boy said, "I'll make you a deal, mister."

The tone of his voice tugged Jack's head around. The two-sided conversation was still going on at the back of the store.

"A *deal*?" queried the outlaw, eyeing the lad quizzically.

"Mm-hm," came the reply. "You see that jar full of hard rock candy up there on the top shelf?"

Jack lifted his gaze in line with the boy's finger. A one-gallon jar sat up there chock-full of candy. It was much higher than the boy could reach. "I see it," he said blandly.

"Fetch me that jar, and I won't holler about the tobacco you stole."

Jack stared at him in disbelief.

"Well, hurry up," urged the lad. "Somebody could come through that door any second. Or Mr. Hanson might show up."

Quickly, the straw-haired outlaw reached up and grasped the jar. He placed it in the boy's waiting hands.

"Thanks, mister." The boy grinned, hugging the jar with both arms. Wheeling, he darted out the door and was gone.

"Why, you little whelp!" Jack breathed, stuffing his own stolen goods in his pockets.

As Jack Taubert moved outside, his eyes strayed to the brick building across the street. A large sign over the door identified it: Bank of El Paso.

Jack thought of the money behind those forbidding walls. He told himself that there would be even more than usual on deposit in the bank with all the extra people in town for the big races tomorrow. For a moment he entertained the idea of pulling a robbery just before closing time the next day. Then he decided against it. He would follow up on Bud Hatch's offer to present him to Turk Killam. Six thousand dollars in eight months was not bad.

Bud Hatch pushed open the door of the Lone Star Stagecoach Company office and stepped inside. Agent Henry Yates was booking passage for a middle-aged man at the counter, and with a short nod of the head, he signaled Hatch toward the back room.

Catching on quickly, Hatch said, "Oh, excuse me. I'm in the wrong place. I wanted the telegraph office."

Backing out the door, Hatch walked among the throng to the nearest corner. He noticed there was a crowd gathered in the street in the next block, where two men were fighting in front of the Tall Texan Saloon.

He made his way down the alley and hastened to the back of the Lone Star office. He found the door unlocked, and looking both ways to make sure no one was watching, he slipped inside. The back room was stifling, and it was apparent that the dusty, flyspecked windows had not been opened in years.

A small table and two chairs were in the middle of the room. On the table stood a full bottle of whiskey and two dirty glasses. Hatch decided he would ignore the heat and enjoy the whiskey. Loosening the cork and pulling it free, he put the bottle to his mouth. After a long pull, he set the bottle down, fought back a burp, and blinked against the sudden rush of water to his eyes.

Hatch could now hear a woman's voice in the front office. He hoped Henry would not be too long; Jack Taubert was not a patient man.

Five minutes later, Henry Yates appeared. "I hung a sign on the front door," he said. "It'll give us a few minutes to talk without being interrupted."

Hatch was in the midst of another pull from the amber-colored bottle. Yates, a small, bald man, took a look at the untouched glasses on the table. "Do you have to drink from the bottle?" he asked, a bit perturbed. "I put the glasses there to drink from."

Hatch ejected a full-grown belch and set the bottle down. "Those glasses are filthy," he objected. "I'm careful about dirt."

"You *should* be more careful about being seen coming here."

"Aw, I forget," said Hatch, shrugging his shoulders. "Besides, with the big crowd in town for the races, who's gonna notice me?"

"Can't be too careful," said Yates. "We don't want this thing messed up. Your boss sure doesn't, and neither do I."

"Okay, I'll be more careful. So what about the gold?"

"The whole sixty thousand is here now. The last of it was brought in from New Mexico two days ago. This time they disguised it by carrying it in an old water wagon. It was placed in the big safe at the Bank of El

Paso under cover of darkness, along with the earlier shipments I already told you about."

Hatch chuckled. "Well, good old Turk will figure a way to get his hands on it."

"It's going to be tougher than you think," the Lone Star agent said advisedly.

"What are you talking about?" asked Hatch, reaching for the whiskey bottle.

"My company hired three Pinkertons to guard the gold. They are with it day and night over there at the bank."

Hatch pulled the bottle from his mouth and sleeved the moisture from his lips. "Turk will be unhappy to hear that," he said with a sigh, "but he won't let the Pinkerton guards stop him. He's going after the gold before it leaves El Paso. He don't want to mess with the army escort that'll be taking it to Austin."

Henry Yates chuckled. "Well, there's where I've got *good* news for your boss. It isn't going with an army escort."

Hatch eyed the little bald-headed man with speculation. "What are you talking about?"

Leaning on the table with his elbows, Henry put his face close to the unshaven features of the outlaw and said, "There's a Texas Ranger on his way from Austin right now. He's coming on horseback."

"Horseback?"

"Yep."

"Why's he doing that? Why doesn't he ride the stage?"

Yates chuckled again. "Because he doesn't want to be seen on the stage. He's coming in at night. He'll tell folks he's from Las Cruces, so nobody will suspect he has anything to do with the gold shipment. The three Pinkerton men got into town without being seen, too. The Ranger and the Pinkertons will appear to be prominent businessmen on their way to Austin."

"Wait a minute," Hatch said, scratching his head. "I'm not following you. It's sounding like these four guys are going to Austin on the stagecoach."

"Exactly." Yates grinned.

"Well, where's the gold gonna be?"

"On the stagecoach."

Hatch's jaw slacked. He stared at the agent as if he did not comprehend what the man was saying. "You're kidding!"

"Nope," said Yates, shaking his head. "The gold will be in regular luggage, riding in the overhead rack."

"Aw, come on, Henry," laughed the outlaw. "You're joshing me. Now what's the real truth?"

"I've just told you the real truth," responded the agent. "Too many army-escorted gold shipments have been plundered by outlaw gangs in these parts lately. The Rangers suggested the stagecoach idea to the company. They bought it."

"Sounds fishy to me," Hatch said flatly. "There's something here that's not stacking up."

"I know it seems odd, Bud," said Yates, rubbing his chin, "but believe me, that's the plan."

"When is the shipment supposed to leave for Austin?" asked the outlaw.

"Won't know until the Ranger arrives. I'm expecting him any day now. Check back with me tomorrow. Once he sets the departure date, your boss can make his plans."

"Okay," said Hatch, rising to his feet. "I'll take the message to Turk, and I'll come by tomorrow."

"To the back door," Yates said, looking at him squarely.

"Yes, of course." Hatch grinned. "To the back door."

Hatch stood up to leave. Rising also, the little man said, "Turk won't forget our deal, will he? I mean about the five thousand for all this information."

Hatch laughed heartily. "Don't you worry about that, Henry, old boy. Turk Killam always pays his debts."

Five minutes later, Bud Hatch entered the cool darkness of the Broken Horseshoe Saloon. Jack Taubert sat alone at a table, smoking a cigarette and sipping from a glass. A whiskey bottle and an extra glass sat on the table next to his sweat-stained hat. There were customers at three other tables, and two men were standing at the bar. One of the saloon women was seated on a man's lap at a corner table, laughing. Two others, freshly painted up, stood talking idly at the end of the bar.

As Hatch threaded his way among the tables to where Jack Taubert was sitting, he caught the eye of one of the women at the end of the bar. Her hair had been henna-dyed a deep reddish brown. She flashed him a warm smile and returned to her conversation.

Slipping into a chair opposite his old prison mate, Hatch said, "Well, pal, looks like a red-hot deal we've had cooking is going to pan out beautiful. I'll take you out to the ranch after we belt down a few and see if Turk will take you into the gang."

Jack's eyes brightened. "Tell me about it, man."

Throwing palms up, Hatch said, "Can't do it, Jack. You know how things are. Once you're in the gang, you'll learn all about it."

Jack nodded, refilling his glass and filling the other glass for Hatch. "I understand," he said evenly.

"Now tell me," said Hatch, picking up the glass and easing back in the chair, "what brings you to El Paso?"

Jack explained that both his parents had died in San Antonio while he was in prison. His younger brother, Tommy, had written to tell him. By the time Jack had been released from prison and made his way home, Tommy had left San Antonio. However, the younger brother had left a message that there had been an inheritance of two thousand dollars from their parents' estate, half of which was Jack's. The older brother was to wait in San Antonio if he wanted his half. Tommy was heading west, and as soon as he settled somewhere, he would send a letter General Delivery informing Jack where he could find him.

"So the letter came six months ago," Jack concluded. "I was gone at the time. Soon as I returned to San Antonio and read the letter, I hotfooted it west. Tommy is punching cattle on a ranch just over the border in New Mexico, about twenty miles the other side of the Franklin Mountains."

"So what were you planning to do after you collect the thousand?"

"Well, until I ran into you, I was heading to Tucson for some excitement. Then I was planning on going to California. Might be some gold left out there somewhere. One way or the other, Bud, old Jack Taubert is going to die a rich man some day. You can bet on it!"

While Hatch was chiding his friend about his unquenchable desire to be rich, his eye caught movement at the bar as the redhead who had smiled at him slipped up close to a tough-looking man who wore a low-slung gun. Drinks were poured, and they stood talking at the bar.

Hatch and Jack Taubert emptied two more glasses while they reminisced about prison. All the while, Hatch kept one eye on the redhead. Finally, she finished her drink, laughed at something the tough-looking man had said, and playfully pulled his hat down over his eyes.

From the corner table, the woman seated on a customer's lap called out, "Hey, Louise!"

The redhead swung her gaze toward the voice. "What is it, Faye?"

"C'mere a minute. Settle an argument between me and Willie, here."

As Louise moved among the tables, her path took her within arm's reach of Bud Hatch. As she drew near, the outlaw reached out, clasping her wrist. She stiffened, but Hatch pulled her down on his lap.

"Ouch!" she protested. "Let go of me!"

"Aw, come on, honey," he guffawed. "I saw the smile you gave me. Now let's be friendly!"

Squirming against his strength, the redhead begged, "Let go of me, mister! Please!"

Jack Taubert smiled at the scene, sipping from his glass.

The man at the bar who had just been talking to the woman turned around slowly and fixed his cold stare on Hatch. "Hey, you!" he roared. "The lady asked you to let go of her. Now do it!"

Hatch turned his whiskey-sodden eyes on the man. Holding Louise tight, he snarled, "You her owner, mister? Huh? Whatever your stinking name is, I don't see it written on her anywhere."

The man's face flushed with anger. He took two steps from the bar, his right hand hovering over the gun on his hip. His jaw muscles bulged, and white tension spots appeared in his cheeks. Through his teeth, he hissed, "Let her go, big mouth. We'll settle this thing right here and now. Or is your liver yellow?"

The patrons of the bar began moving toward the walls. The bartender edged out of the line of fire. Jack Taubert scooted his chair back and stood up, throwing the man a hot glare.

"Forget it, Jack," said Hatch, releasing the trembling woman. "I'll handle it."

Jack did not budge as Louise skittered away.

Hatch stood up slowly, his hand splayed over his gun. He was unsteady from the effects of the whiskey.

Keeping his eyes on the man, Jack said to Hatch, "You're drunk, Bud. Don't try to match his gun."

"I'm not drunk, old pal," argued Hatch. "I can handle this dude."

Speaking to Hatch's challenger, Jack said, "Look, whatever your name is, you can see he's too drunk to face you. He let the woman go. Now let's forget the whole thing. Come and sit down. We'll have a drink together."

"I don't drink with women maulers like him or scummy long-haired trash like you," lashed the man, stormy eyed. "He was sober enough to smart mouth me. He's sober enough to go for his gun."

The smell of death filled the room. Without hesitation, Bud Hatch clawed for the weapon in his holster.

His challenger was fast. He let Hatch's muzzle appear before his own hand darted downward. The gun was out and spitting fire before Hatch could pull his trigger.

In the same instant, Jack Taubert drew and fired, sending a bullet into the man's chest.

The women screamed as Hatch sagged to the floor. The other man stumbled backward from the impact of Jack's bullet. When his back hit the bar, he fell to the floor and lay still. His eyes were wide and bulging, but seemed to see nothing.

Figuring him to be dead, Jack turned his attention toward his fallen friend. Suddenly, there was a scraping noise behind him. Jack whirled. The man's sightless eyes were alive again. With one last effort, he raised his gun, lining it on Jack's midsection.

The straw-haired outlaw leveled his gun while his adversary was struggling to thumb back the hammer of his quivering weapon. Jack Taubert's gun roared, and a black hole centered the man's forehead. He flopped back, never to move again.

Jack holstered his smoking gun and knelt beside the semiconscious Bud Hatch. Blood was spreading around the hole in his chest.

Heavy footsteps were heard on the boardwalk. The doors swung open, and Deputy Marshal Daryl Dunn appeared. Dunn was a tall man in his late twenties. Hastening to the sprawled-out gunslinger, he saw instantly that the man was dead. He swung his gaze to where Jack Taubert knelt beside the wounded Bud Hatch. Then he looked at the bartender. "What happened, Clete?"

Cletus Holcomb, the saloon's proprietor and bartender, told the deputy exactly what had happened to Bud Hatch, including the fact that the skinny man with the long yellow hair had tried to stop the gunplay. Other witnesses confirmed it, one adding that Jack had no choice in gunning the man down.

Dunn accepted it, stepping to where Hatch lay in a half-conscious state, breathing heavily. "This man your friend?" Dunn asked Jack Taubert.

Jack looked up and nodded. "Yeah. Is there a doctor in this town?"

"Yes," replied the deputy. "Let's get him over to Doc Finch's office down the street."

The two men hurriedly carried Hatch to the doctor's office under the gawking eyes of the crowd on the street. Arriving at the office, they found a handwritten note on the door:

At Jim Bandy's barber shop getting a haircut.
Will return shortly. Door to outer office is
unlocked.

                            Aaron K. Finch, M.D.

There was no one in the place. The two men laid
Hatch on a couch in the outer office, and then Dunn
rushed out the door, saying he would run and get the
doctor.

Jack pulled up a chair and looked into the eyes of his
dying friend. "Hang on, Bud," he said in an encourag-
ing tone. "We'll have the doctor here in a minute."

Hatch coughed, wincing with pain. "Ain't no use,
Jack. I ain't gonna . . . make it." He coughed again.
"Listen. I . . . I . . . gotta tell you something. You'll
have to take . . . the message to Turk."

Quickly, Hatch told Jack of the sixty-thousand-dollar
gold shipment and filled him in on the information he
had received from Henry Yates.

Reaching up with his trembling fingers and grasping
Jack's shirt collar, he coughed and said, "You . . . you
will tell Turk, won't you?"

"Sure. Sure I will." Jack nodded. "Where's his place?"

"Six . . . six miles due . . . west of the Franklins.
Has . . . has a lot of cottonwoods . . . around the house
and . . . buildings. Thick with black angus and . . .
Texas . . . Texas longhorns. Has . . . Killam name
right . . . on the gate."

Jack started to speak, when Hatch jerked, coughed,
and went limp. He was gone.

Seconds later, the deputy and Dr. Aaron Finch hurried through the door. Jack stood up to meet them.
"He's dead, gentlemen," he said levelly.

"Daryl told me about the shooting," said Finch. "You
two been friends long?"

"A few years. We knew each other in east Texas."

The deputy spoke up. "I'll need you to sign a statement on the shooting for me, Mr.—"

"Uh . . . Taubert," said Jack, wondering instantly if

he should have given the lawman his real name. Then he shrugged it off. Why not? He was not running from the law at the moment. "Jack Taubert, Deputy."

Leaving Bud Hatch's body with the doctor, Jack accompanied Dunn to the marshal's office and signed the necessary statement. Then elbowing his way through the crowded street, he swung into the saddle and headed for the river. Riding the north bank westward, he skirted the southern tip of the Franklin Mountains.

As Jack Taubert rode toward Turk Killam's ranch, he thought about the gold in the safe at the Bank of El Paso. The sixty thousand dollars loomed large in his avaricious mind, and the greed in his blood began to surface. One way or another, he had to have that gold.

The miles passed slowly as a plan began to form. There was no way he could pull off the robbery by himself. It would take more than one man to get past those three Pinkerton guards Bud Hatch had told him about. It was going to take a team of robbers to get the gold out of that safe and away from El Paso.

Jack decided he would work his way into the Killam gang and be in on the robbery. Once the gold was in the hands of the gang and out of town, he would find a way to take the gold all for himself. He would then light out for Tucson.

The rapacious outlaw knew it was not going to be easy to rob the Killam bunch of the gold. But for Jack Taubert, where there was a will—and money to be had—there was a way.

Chapter Four

The sun was setting behind the rugged, barren Franklin Mountains as Ranger Branson Howard topped a hill east of El Paso. The tough border town lay peacefully in the deep shadows of the mountains. Halting Herb Nolan's blue roan, the Ranger ran his gaze in a panorama, taking in the awesome scene. The land looked like burnished gold in the flame of the sunset.

Behind him to the east lay the dry salt flats through which he had just passed. To the north were the sun-bleached badlands of New Mexico. To the south was Old Mexico, her hazy purple mountains reaching for the reddening sky in the distance. The sun's slanting rays illuminated Mexico's broad, sweeping valleys in a golden light. Separating the two countries as a natural border was the lazy Rio Grande River below.

The Rio Grande appeared at that moment as a gleaming ribbon of molten fire, winding its way across the magnificent sunburnt land. The river was flanked by the town of El Paso del Norte on the Mexican side to the south, and by El Paso on the American side to the north.

The Texas Ranger left the saddle and walked about, stretching his legs. He would wait and ride into El Paso after dark, so as to be as inconspicuous as possible. He did not mind being seen before taking the gold shipment to Austin, but the less he was noticed, the better. Once he was in town among the people, he would be just another face in the crowd. The main thing was to ride in without attracting undue attention.

At that moment, a movement caught his eye southward toward the bottom of the hill. There was the Concord stagecoach from Austin, dusting along like a square-hulled boat on a choppy sea. This was the stage the Ranger would be taking back to Austin in two days. Branson could barely hear the rumble of the hooves of the six-horse team or the rattle of the rocking vehicle.

He pushed the broad-brimmed Stetson to the back of his head as he followed the coach with his gaze. That would be Sam Neff at the reins. Sam was tough as boot leather and well seasoned. He had driven the Austin—El Paso run ever since the Lone Star Stagecoach Company had opened it. Branson did not know the shotgunner.

While he watched the sun relinquish its reign to the gathering night, Branson again pondered his assignment. If everything was on schedule, the full shipment of gold nuggets was now safely resting in El Paso. He pictured the three Pinkerton men cooped up in the bank sitting in front of the huge vault and waiting for his arrival.

Branson chuckled. He would like to have seen the three as they transported the fortune from the New Mexico mountains to El Paso little by little, wearing different disguises—ranchers, drifters, drummers, mule skinners.

Branson had been in constant touch with Frank Rainey by stagecoach mail, giving the bank president precise instructions on the delivery and safekeeping of the gold. The shipment was top secret, known only to the Texas Rangers, the town's two lawmen, the stage crew, the five employees of the bank, the Lone Star Stagecoach Company officials in Austin, and Henry Yates, the Lone Star agent in El Paso.

Calculating carefully, Branson had figured the sixty thousand dollars in gold nuggets would weigh just about an even two hundred pounds. He had instructed Frank Rainey to have it placed in eight canvas bags of twenty-five pounds each. The bags would be packed into four ordinary suitcases, making it easy to load the gold into the rack on top of the coach.

The Ranger entertained some additional thoughts on making the transportation of the gold safer, as the faint red light of the dying sun grew darker and darker. Finally, the red hue turned black, like blood when it settles in sand.

Under cover of darkness, Branson Howard guided the blue roan off the hill northward. He would swing around and ride into El Paso from the north. To anyone who saw him, this would jibe with his claim to have ridden in from Las Cruces.

As the horse picked its way downward in the dark, the Ranger eyed the winking lights of the town. There was a fortune in gold down there in their midst. He felt the weight of his responsibility.

El Paso was alive with people as Branson rode in and moved southward down Stanton Street. Music and laughter emanated from the saloons as he turned west onto San Francisco Street. The saloon sounds commingled with the shouts and other noises along the well-lit street. If anyone noticed the lone rider, they did not show it.

The races always brought people from miles around. It was El Paso's gala annual affair, and both the Americans and the Mexicans made the most of it. The town's residents would get little sleep tonight, thanks to the carousers who would be out on the streets until dawn.

The Ranger rode west, setting his gaze on the jagged Franklins, dark and ghostly against the star-studded sky. Reaching Durango Street, he turned left and found the bank president's house at the far corner of the block.

Swinging stiffly from the saddle, Branson walked across the porch and rapped on the door. Light footsteps were heard, and then the door came open. A small, silver-haired woman held a lantern in her hand. Raising it to spray its light on the muscular man's face, she said, "Oh, it's you, Captain Howard. Come in. Frank was saying at supper this evening that you should be showing up soon."

"It's nice to see you, Mrs. Rainey." The Ranger smiled, removing his broad-brimmed Stetson and stepping inside.

"Frank is in the library, Captain," she said, returning the smile. "You know where it is. He will be glad to know you are here. Have you eaten? You look tired."

"It's been a long, hard trip, ma'am," he replied amiably. "I haven't eaten yet this evening, but I plan to do that after I check in at the hotel."

"Why don't I just fire up the stove and fix you a good home-cooked meal?"

"That's awfully nice of you, Mrs. Rainey." Branson grinned. "But I really can't stay that long. I have to see the Lone Star agent as soon as I talk to your husband. Thank you, anyway."

The banker's wife stepped into the kitchen, and Branson Howard walked down a long hallway and entered the library. Frank Rainey was hunched over a desk working on some papers as the Texas Ranger entered the room. A pipe was clenched between Rainey's teeth. He looked up and a broad smile spread across his face. He stood and extended his hand. "Ah, Captain Howard. I'm glad you're here. Long, hot trip, eh?"

"That's for sure," replied the Ranger, meeting his grasp.

The two men sat down in plush, overstuffed horse-hair chairs, facing each other. The banker placed a glass of brandy in the Ranger's hand.

"The full sixty thousand is here, ready for shipment," volunteered Rainey. "Pinkerton men are waiting for you."

"Good," said Branson. "Looks like we're operating on schedule. I'll talk to Henry Yates and make sure everything is set for the trip to Austin. My plans are to head out Thursday, but first I want to talk to the driver about some extra precautionary measures." Standing up, he finished the brandy, and added, "Thanks for all your help, sir. I really appreciate it."

The silver-haired banker nodded. "Glad to oblige,

Captain. But isn't two days a pretty short time for you
to rest up?"

"I'll be fine." Branson grinned. "They tell every Texas
Ranger when he signs on that he will have to wait till
he retires to rest."

Rainey chuckled. "You don't have banker's hours,
that's for sure."

While walking Branson to the door, the banker told
him that room 9 was reserved for him at the Rio Grande
Hotel. The business suit that he had been measured
for, the last time he was in town, was in the room,
along with a new gray Stetson. He would certainly look
the part of a prominent businessman.

The Ranger rode back to San Francisco Street, passed
the Lone Star office, swung into the alley, and dismounted at the back door. Henry Yates responded to
his knock and invited him upstairs to his living quar-
ters, where the two men discussed the details of the
gold shipment. So far, everything was going as planned.

Yates was unaware of Bud Hatch's death. Thinking
that the outlaw would return the next day for news of
the planned date of departure, he asked Branson Howard and was glad to learn that it was just two days away.
All of this sneaking about had been playing on his
nerves. He would be glad to get it over with and pocket
his share of the gold.

Branson reminded Yates that for safety's sake, he
should book no passengers on the Austin-bound stage
other than himself and the three Pinkerton men. He
stressed the importance of everything looking normal.
Yates assured him that it would be so.

Finally, Branson told Yates about killing the two
outlaws at the oasis and their planned rendezvous with
Vic Barry. Not wanting to give away his cover, he asked
Yates to wire the Ranger headquarters in Austin so that
they could arrange for some of their agents to try to
apprehend Barry.

Leaving the Lone Star office, the Ranger checked the
roan in at a livery stable down the street from the hotel,
threw the saddlebags over his shoulder, and headed up

the boardwalk. As he drew abreast of the Longhorn
Saloon, the flailing body of a man came tumbling through
the swinging doors, rolled off the boardwalk, and landed
in the street. Directly behind him, a thick-bodied, bull-
necked man thundered through the saloon door, cursing violently. Several more followed the big man, eager
to watch the show.

The Ranger saw instantly that the man rolling in the
dust was quite small and showed signs of being somewhere in his late fifties. He was frail and wore a red-and-
white striped shirt with sleeve garters. It was evident
the big man outweighed him by well over a hundred
pounds and was half his age.

"Bash his brains out, Horace!" yelled one of the
onlookers as the big man hoisted the small one to his
feet.

"Pick him up and slam him on the ground, Perky!"
cried another, mocking the little man.

Horace was swearing at little Perky and shaking him
savagely. Branson Howard waited for someone to step
in and stop it. He was reluctant to do so, not wanting to
draw attention to himself.

The little man's neck looked like it would snap under
the strength of the brute. Fear and pain showed in his
thin face. Apparently no one was going to put a halt to
the brutality.

As Horace drew back his fist, ready to punch the
smaller man, Branson Howard shoved his way through
the crowd, shouting, "Hey! Hold it right there!"

Horace held his fist cocked and looked around to see
who owned the voice. Branson still carried the saddlebags over one shoulder. Moving up close, he looked the
big man in the eye and said, "Shame on you, Horace,
picking on a little man twice your age."

Squinting, Horace said, "Do I know you?"

"Nope."

"Then, how come you know my name?"

Gesturing toward the crowd, the Ranger said, "Your
bloodthirsty pals here have been shouting it. Now let
him go."

Horace gave him a bone-dry look. "You gonna make me?"

Branson's hazel eyes suddenly looked like chipped ice. "If I have to."

"You just butt out, mister," Horace said with a raw edge to his voice. "This is none of your business."

"It *will* be, if you don't let go of him," rasped the Texas Ranger. "What's your beef, anyway?"

Still holding his fist cocked, Horace replied, "This little twerp plays the piano in there. He sang a song in front of everybody, makin' fun of me."

"I did not, mister!" protested Perky to the Ranger. "I was singing a song about a cockeyed horse, and every time I said *horse*, he thought I was saying *Horace*. He's just got a big ol' chip on his shoulder."

"You're lyin', piano player!" snarled the big man. "You were makin' fun of me!"

"You're acting like a fool, Horace," Branson said icily. "Let him go."

Horace set his jaw and said through clenched teeth, "I let go of him when you step up here and take his place."

Branson slipped the saddlebags from his shoulder and stepped up close. The big man released the piano player and faced the muscular Ranger, balling his fists.

Extending the saddlebags to the little man, Branson said, "Here, Perky, hold these for me."

Perky took them and stepped away. Horace's huge right fist was already coming. Like a wicked club, it caught Branson Howard behind the left ear.

Branson felt his knees go soggy as the impact shot through his head. The ground flew up and struck him in the face. Horace's friends ejected a rousing cheer. For a moment, they sounded distant to the Ranger. His head was buzzing. Suddenly he felt a battering ram slam him in the rib cage. The pain instantly cleared his head, and he realized the battering ram was the big man's boot. It was coming again.

Branson rolled in the nick of time, and the boot whistled past him. Instinct, spawned by a hundred similar fights, caused him to reach out with both hands and grasp the big foot. He wrenched it savagely. Horace howled and fell down hard, cursing his opponent.

The Ranger bounded to his feet, favoring his left side. His ribs felt like they were on fire. Branson knew he would have to ignore the pain and fight.

Horace got up and came at him like an enraged bull, both fists pumping. The muscular Ranger sidestepped, letting him charge past. Then he kicked him hard in the rump. The big man was already limping on a twisted ankle. He stumbled and fell.

Branson was now aware of an enlarged crowd, a good number of which were cheering him.

The last move had embarrassed Horace. Swearing at the Ranger, he growled, "I'm gonna knock your head off!"

Taunting him to make him madder, Branson said, "You do it, then talk about it."

Horace thundered in again. The thick-shouldered Ranger set himself, timed his punch, and caught the big man solidly on the jaw. The impact sent a shock all the way to Branson Howard's ankles.

Horace's feet left the ground as he fell onto his back. Rolling to his knees, the huge man struggled to get up. The Ranger stood over him, saying, "Stay down, Horace, and it's all over."

"Can't do it," mumbled Horace, clambering unsteadily to his feet. "I started this. I'm gonna finish it!" While he spoke, he swung wildly.

The Ranger dodged and then drove a punch to his nose. Horace shook his head, and Branson doubled him over with a violent blow to the midsection. Horace hovered there for a moment, eyes glazed, his face a perfect target. Bracing his feet, the Ranger brought in a punch that connected with sledgehammer force.

Horace dropped unconscious to the wagon-rutted street. While Horace's friends hurried to him, Branson stepped to the grateful piano player, accepted the saddlebags from his trembling fingers, and left the scene.

Entering the lobby of the Rio Grande Hotel, Branson

was greeted with a smile by the clerk. While signing the register, he noticed that Sam Neff was in room 2.

The Ranger was hungrier than ever after his workout with Horace, but business had to come first tonight. Depositing the saddlebags in room 9, he retraced his steps down the hallway and rapped on the door of number 2.

The door came open to reveal the bearded fifty-year-old face of Sam Neff. Grinning broadly as he recognized the lawman, he exclaimed, "Branson Howard! You handsome scalawag! Come on in here!"

The two men shook hands as the door went closed behind them. Another man, in his early forties, was also in the room. Neff said, "Branson, I'd like you to meet my new shotgunner, Ray Ringdon."

"Hello, Ray," said Branson, grasping his hand.

"Mighty glad to finally meet you, Captain," said Ringdon, smiling. "Sam's told me a lot about you. Of course, I've known your name for years. In fact, I actually saw you once."

"Oh?" Branson's eyebrows raised.

"Yeah. Down in Del Rio. The day Earl Tanner challenged you."

The Ranger nodded slowly, his features showing distaste of the memory.

"You should've seen him, Sam," said Ringdon, shaking his head in amazement. "Tanner was supposed to be greased lightning on the draw. Ha! Mr. Howard made him look like sick molasses! Tanner didn't even clear leather before he was deader'n Aunt Matilda's doorknob!"

Sam Neff observed that Branson Howard was uncomfortable with Ringdon's line of conversation. Changing the subject, Neff said, "You stayin' here at the hotel, Branson?"

"Yes. Room 9, down the hall. I just came in."

"Sounded like there was a big fight a few minutes ago out there on the street, Captain," piped up the shotgunner. "Did you see it?"

"Yeah," responded Branson. "From right up close."

Turning to the stage driver, he said, "Sam, it looks like we'll pull out for Austin on Thursday morning, as planned."

"Good."

Branson impressed upon the two men the importance of secrecy in the entire operation. They were not to show they knew him when out in public, and they were to keep all they knew about the gold to themselves.

"I agree, Branson," said Neff. "Sixty thousand dollars is a lot of money. We can't be too careful. Outlaws have strange ways of smelling large fortunes."

"You're right on that count," agreed the Ranger. "Both of you sit down here for a minute. Sam, there is something I want you and Ray to do as an extra precaution. . . ."

Chapter Five

At midafternoon that same day, outlaws Bill Storey and Hugh Pyle were pulling into the yard of the Turk Killam ranch with a load of hay. The heavily loaded wagon groaned as Storey guided it past the house. The left rear wheel was wobbling dangerously, about to come off.

"Take it real easy, Bill," Pyle said, leaning from the seat as he attempted to see the wheel underneath the overhanging hay. "Just about fifty yards and we'll be to the feed trough."

Storey turned his face toward the open door of the long, low ranch house. The sound of a heavy voice came from the dark interior, spewing profanity.

"Sounds like Turk is on the rampage again," mused Storey.

"Do you mean again or still?" Pyle chuckled. "Seems to me he's never off the rampage."

Bill Storey raised his hat, sleeved away the sweat, and dropped the hat back in place. "Well, you're catching on, Hugh. How long have you been with us now?"

"Almost three weeks."

"You'll learn the truth of your statement as time goes by," said Storey. "I've worked for the old boy for five years. It's like he's got a permanent burr stuck in the trapdoor of his long johns."

As the wagon moved slowly past the house, Pyle's gaze fell on a huge man chopping wood beside a small building up ahead that served as a woodshed. He watched the man swinging the ax, splitting each log with one easy blow.

Shaking his head, Pyle said, "Bill, that cousin of yours is stronger'n a grizzly bear, I swear."

"I can tell you things he's done that'll stagger your imagination," boasted Storey. "It's like he's got the strength of a bull elephant in each arm. That's why Turk lets me keep him around. He's plenty useful around a place like this."

Clearing his throat, Hugh Pyle set his eyes momentarily on Storey and said, "I don't want to embarrass you or nothing, but has his thinking . . . well, I mean . . . has Ernie always been—"

"Slow?" asked Storey, finishing his question for him.

"Well . . . yeah."

"Yes." Storey nodded. "Ernie was born—"

Suddenly the left rear wheel of the wagon came off the axle. The wagon sagged and plowed dirt as Storey pulled the horses to a halt. Hugh Pyle swore.

Both men slid to the ground and examined the situation. The wagon was tilted precariously, but the overhanging hay remained surprisingly in place. Storey eyed the axle. "Nothing broken," he said.

Pyle swore again and then looked up, gauging the distance to the feeding trough. "Another sixty feet, and we'd have made it," he said dejectedly. "Now we gotta fork this whole load all the way over to the trough."

"Maybe not," said Storey, standing up. "All we need is to jack the wagon up. We can slip the wheel back on."

"Sure," laughed Pyle. "And of course you've got a house jack in your hip pocket!"

"Something better than that." Storey grinned. Looking past Pyle, he set his gaze on Ernie Carpenter, who was now picking up the wood he had chopped. "Hey, Ernie!" he called.

The enormous twenty-one-year-old man turned slowly, setting his eyes on Storey. A pleasant smile spread over his wide face. "Hullo, Cousin Bill," he said, slurring the words. "What do you want?"

"Come here and I'll show you!"

Ernie bent down slowly, laying the logs in a neat

pile, as a child would lay his toy building blocks. Rising to his full height of six feet seven inches, he shuffled toward the stranded hay wagon.

Hugh Pyle studied the massive man. Ernie had an extra-large head, even for his immense body. His shaggy, light-brown hair dangled loosely over his forehead. He had a broad nose, a wide mouth, and thick lips. He was thick of body, with huge sloping shoulders.

Drawing close, Ernie gave Storey his simple smile and said, "What's the matter, Cousin Bill? Is the wagon broke?"

"The wheel came off," responded Storey. "We need to put it back on so the horses can pull the wagon over to the feed trough, there by the corral fence."

Ernie turned slowly, looking toward the corral. Several head of cattle stood idly inside the pole fence. Turning back, he said in his slow manner, "The cows are hungry, huh?"

"Yes," said Storey. "Now, Ernie, we need you to lift up this corner of the wagon so we can put the wheel back on. Okay?"

Hugh Pyle eyed Storey in disbelief. "Hey, come on, Bill. That load of hay will weigh a ton or better. The weight on this corner would be six or seven hundred pounds. There ain't any one man gonna lift it an inch, let alone high enough to put the wheel back on!"

Ernie turned his torpid, gray eyes on the newest outlaw in the gang. "I can do it, mister—" He rubbed his forehead. "Uh . . . mister . . . I forgot your name."

"It's Hugh Pyle," spoke up Bill Storey.

"Oh, sure." Ernie nodded. Patting Pyle's shoulder gently while towering over him, he said, "I can lift the wagon, Mr. Hugh. Don't you worry none."

While Ernie backed himself against the tilting vehicle and gripped the corner of the bed beneath the overhanging hay, Storey and Pyle knelt down and took hold of the wheel. When it was in the proper position, Storey said, "Okay, Ernie."

Hugh Pyle's mouth gaped as Ernie Carpenter hoisted

the wagon with little strain showing. Quickly, the wheel went into place.

"All right, Ernie," said Storey. "Set it down."

The big man did so and then mumbled something about getting the wood into the house as he scuffed his way back to the pile of logs.

Pyle watched him go, shaking his head. "I never would have believed it!"

Bill Storey climbed up in the driver's seat. "I told you he's got the strength of a bull elephant. Just don't ever get him mad at you."

Looking in the direction Ernie had gone, Pyle said, "He seems so gentle. It's hard to picture him angry."

"He can get that way." Ernie's cousin grinned. "When he does, he's dangerous."

"Anything particular set him off?" asked Pyle, walking beside the wagon as Storey clucked to the horses and guided them toward the feed trough.

"He can't stand to see animals abused," Storey answered. "We have to make sure Ernie is not around when we shoe the horses or brand the cattle. He goes berserk if he thinks you're hurting them."

"I'll be sure to be kind to animals around him." Pyle chuckled.

"But Ernie's fuse is really short," continued Storey, "when it comes to Miss Lucy. He hovers over her like an old mother hen. Nobody better mistreat her when he is around."

"How about the way Turk treats her?" queried Pyle. "You'd think she was his cur dog sometimes."

"You'll notice that Turk only gets rough with Miss Lucy when Ernie isn't around," said Storey, pulling the wagon alongside the pole fence next to the feed trough. "Turk has a healthy respect for Ernie's power." Standing in the seat and climbing on top of the hay with pitchfork in hand, he added, "There have been a few times when Turk has forgotten Ernie was close and roughed her up. I've had to jump in quick. Only Ernie's respect for me has saved Turk."

Hugh Pyle climbed up and began helping the tall,

dark-headed Storey pitch hay into the feed trough. Immediately, the cattle began gathering to the area.

To satisfy his curiosity, Pyle asked, "How much does Ernie weigh, Bill?"

"He's right around three hundred pounds. All brawn, too."

"You started to say something about when he was born, when the wagon broke down."

"Oh, yes." Storey nodded. "You asked if he had always been slow. He was born that way. His mother, my ma's sister, died giving him birth. Ernie weighed sixteen pounds. Aunt Leah Carpenter's husband had died only a month before the baby was born. My mother, Lila Storey, was the midwife at Ernie's birth. She was able to save him, but not my aunt. There was no one else to take him, so we kept him with us."

"So your parents raised him, huh?"

"My mother, mostly," replied Storey. "Pa died when Ernie was three. I was ten. She raised us, along with my three sisters."

Tossing a forkful of hay over the fence, Pyle asked, "When did you take to the outlaw trail?"

"Ma died when I was sixteen. My sisters were already married and gone. There wasn't any money, so I took to stealing and robbing. Got pretty good at it. Then Turk came along, and I've been working for him ever since. When he made the deal, I told him Ernie would have to come along. There's no one else to take care of him."

Inside the huge ranch house, Turk Killam stormed, swore, and snorted like an angry bull. He paced the floor, with his face in a cloud of cigar smoke, angry at Bud Hatch for tarrying so long in El Paso.

"That sot is probably lying under a table in one of the saloons," fumed Killam. "I should've known better than to send him into town. He should've been back here two hours ago."

The fifty-year-old outlaw leader had a deep voice that

resembled the rumble of thunder when he was angry. He was a broad, thick-bodied man, standing five-feet-eight inches and weighing just over two hundred pounds. He had an ugly, raw-red face that flushed to deep crimson during his temper fits.

Killam's bushy black hair was flecked with silver, and it dangled loosely over a square forehead that bottomed out in thick, tangled eyebrows over deep-set, widely spaced black eyes. The eyebrows grew together, leaving no space between them, above his wide, flat nose. The lower part of his face was half-masked by a heavy beard and mustache that were more gray than black.

The hot-tempered outlaw leader was greedy, vicious, and heartless. He would stop at nothing to satisfy his own rapacious desires.

Killam's anger was boiling now because he was eager to learn from Bud Hatch if all the gold was in El Paso and ready to be shipped to Austin. Only Lone Star agent Henry Yates could supply the needed information. Without it, Killam could not proceed with his plans to steal the sixty-thousand-dollar shipment.

While the bearded outlaw leader paced and chewed his cigar, other faces were evident in the room. Slouching in a pair of overstuffed chairs and smoking cigarettes were gang members Al Weems and Dirk Holstead.

In one corner of the large room was a narrow bed set up on a wooden platform, making the level of the mattress four feet from the floor. The bed had been positioned this high to make it easier to care for Killam's invalid wife.

Dorothy Killam had been thrown by a horse some six years previously, and her spinal column had been injured severely, leaving her paralyzed below the waist. Her neck had also been damaged, and her condition was such that any sudden movement or jolt could instantly paralyze her from the neck down. A fall could snap the spine and kill her.

Thus it was impossible for Dorothy to be moved from the ranch by horseback or by wagon. She would remain in that very bed until the day she died.

Sitting beside Dorothy's bed was her twenty-three-year-old daughter, Lucy Daniels. Lucy had long, jet-black hair that framed a strikingly beautiful face. Killam's men would eye her from a distance, admiring her form and beauty, but afraid to make advances toward her because of Ernie Carpenter.

Lucy had eyes the color of blue velvet. They were alert, gentle, and compassionate. However, they carried a sober shadow. The beautiful young woman was a virtual prisoner; she could not leave her helpless mother.

There was bad blood between Lucy Daniels and her brutal stepfather. Turk Killam treated her like a slave and often manhandled her when Ernie was not around. Periodically she bore bruises from his beatings.

Chewing his cigar and puffing smoke like a locomotive, Turk Killam continued swearing and pacing the floor. One thing everybody in the room knew for sure—Bud Hatch was in for it whenever he did show up.

Dorothy Killam lay on the slender bed, her dark hair contrasting with the pallor of her face. Deep lines furrowed her brow. Rolling her head carefully on the pillow, she said, "Turk, I wish you wouldn't use that kind of language in front of Lucy. I've asked you before not to do it."

Killam stopped, pulled the cigar from his mouth, and looked across the room at his invalid wife. His only soft spot was for her. "Aw, Dorothy," he bawled, "Lucy's heard cussing before. Ain't gonna hurt her none. Besides, I'm mad!"

Lucy eyed her stepfather blandly. With disdain in her voice, she said, "Anger is no excuse. Profanity is just an indication of a painfully limited vocabulary. Even if my presence means nothing to you, Turk, you ought to keep your mouth clean in respect for my mother."

Killam's red face grew deeper in color. The blaze in his wide-set eyes grew hotter. Stomping to where Lucy sat, he looked down at her and growled, "When I want advice out of you, I'll slap it out, do you hear me?"

Lucy stared back at him, unmoved.

Dorothy whimpered, "Please don't hit her, Turk!"

At the same instant, Ernie Carpenter's familiar skidding footsteps sounded on the porch outside.

"Boss!" spoke up Al Weems.

Killam pivoted, throwing his hard glance through the open door. The huge man's hulking frame filled the doorway as he entered, carrying a load of chopped wood. Ernie looked past Killam at Lucy and smiled as he moved into the kitchen and deposited the logs beside the big iron stove.

Reappearing, Ernie shuffled his way toward the door, smiling at the brunette beauty and saying, "I chopped a whole lot of wood for you, Miss Lucy. Now you can cook lots and lots of suppers. There's more at the woodshed. I'll be back with it in a minute."

"Thank you, Ernie," said Lucy, returning the smile.

Ernie gave Turk Killam a cautious look, wondering why he was standing over Lucy. Allowing his dull gaze to move back to Lucy, he asked, "Is something wrong, Miss Lucy?"

"Not now, Ernie. Mr. Killam and I were just having a little talk. You run along and get the rest of the wood."

"All right," Ernie said slowly, giving Killam a suspicious look as he ambled out the door.

Killam returned to his pacing, once again cursing Bud Hatch.

Attempting to ease the tension, Dirk Holstead spoke up with a note of cheer in his voice. "Hey, boss, would you like for me to saddle up and ride into town? I can be there and back in no time. I'll see Yates and get the lowdown. If I can find Bud, I'll throw him over the back of his horse and bring him home."

Killam's cigar had gone out. While lighting it again, he puffed hard and said, "I gave the job to Bud. He'd just better do it. I'm giving him till sundown. If he ain't here by then, *I'm* going after him. He'll be one sorry sot if I have to do it." With that, the bearded outlaw leader resumed his pacing.

Outside, Ernie Carpenter made his way to the woodshed and was about to pick up another load of wood when he realized he had a lump in his right shoe. Sitting down on the ground, he untied the laces and methodically removed it. Turning the huge high-top shoe upside down, he watched a tiny pebble roll out. Picking up the pebble, he examined it closely for several moments.

Not far away, Bill Storey and Hugh Pyle were finishing unloading the wagon. Pyle took the team to the barn to remove the harnesses, and Storey headed toward the house. As he drew near the woodshed, he spied his cousin sitting on the ground in his bib overalls, attempting to tie his shoe.

"Having trouble, big boy?" queried Storey.

"I ain't never gonna learn to make a bowknot," the big man said dejectedly.

"Sure you are." Storey smiled, kneeling down. "Here, let me show you one more time."

Five minutes later, as the cousins carried wood toward the house, Ernie said, "Cousin Bill, I think I'm gonna hurt Mr. Turk."

Concern etched itself immediately on Storey's face. "Why do you say that?"

"Because he's not being nice to Miss Lucy. I think he was being bad to her again a little while ago, when I went into the house. I'm gonna hurt him, Cousin Bill."

"Now, Ernie, listen to me," said Storey, putting a note of authority in his voice. "You and I need to work for Mr. Killam so we can have a place to live and food to eat. You must never hurt him. You must treat him nice and never make him angry. He and Miss Lucy are family. It is not our business what they do."

Shaking his head as they approached the porch, Ernie said, "I can't let him be bad to her."

Inside the house, Turk Killam had decided he wanted a drink of whiskey. Going to a cupboard in the kitchen, he had found that the last whiskey bottle had been drained. Returning to the large living room, he said to Lucy, "Go to the cellar and get me a bottle of whiskey."

Standing up, the dark-eyed woman said, "It's time

for me to give Mother her rubdown. Go get the whiskey yourself. It will take your mind off of Bud."

Anger flared afresh in Turk Killam. He stomped to Lucy, who stood only three inches shorter than himself, and blew a cloud of smoke in her face.

Ernie was just coming in the door with his load of wood, followed by his cousin. Killam's present action had drawn everyone's attention, and they had not noticed the cousins coming.

Killam, again blowing smoke in Lucy's face, was blaring, "Don't you smart mouth me, girl! I told you what to do, now you do it!"

Ernie's heavy jaw slacked as he took in the scene. Anger claimed him. Dropping the cut logs on the floor, he headed for Turk Killam with blood in his dull eyes.

Chapter Six

Jack Taubert held his horse to a brisk walk as he skirted the southern tip of the barren Franklin Mountains. In the distance, sunshine danced on the surface of the lazy Rio Grande.

Continuing westward, the skinny outlaw entertained blissful thoughts of soon heading toward California with the sixty thousand dollars in gold nuggets in his possession. The first thing to do was get his hands on his share of the inheritance from Tommy. This would give him some money for expenses until he was able to convert the gold nuggets to cash. Then Jack would put his eager, greedy brain to work. He would find a way to separate the Killam gang from the gold, once they had stolen it from the Lone Star stage.

As Jack left the Franklin Mountains behind, his eyes took in the broad, sweeping land ahead. He could make out the long, spruce-topped mesas in the distance, lying flat and still under the azure New Mexico sky. Along the river were small homesteads, punctuated with brown stacks of wild hay and criss-crossed pole fences. A dark green strip five hundred yards wide fringed both sides of the river.

Yellow clumps of snakeweed dotted the desert floor, amid scattered prickly poppy, long-fingered ocotillo shrub, patches of purple-tinged pear cactus, and the ever-present sagebrush. The dry, brown-grassed plain lay quietly baking in the afternoon sun.

The wind came up, throwing its hot breath against the yellow-haired rider. A dust devil scooped up a

handful of gritty sand and threw it in his face. He swore
and spit, thumbing the stinging matter from his eyes.

The blazing sun was dropping toward the western
horizon when Jack approached the gate of the Killam
ranch. Bud Hatch was right—the place couldn't be
missed. The outlaw leader's name was emblazoned in
large white letters on a flat board attached to the gate.

Leaning from the saddle, Jack lifted the wire loop
that held the gate to a post and swung it open. He
guided his mount through the wide opening and then
closed the gate.

As he rode the quarter mile toward the house and
outbuildings that were set in a cluster of towering cottonwood trees, he marveled at the clever cover-up.
Here were several hundred head of fat beef stock moving about sluggishly in the lowering sun. The place was
quiet and peaceful. No one would ever guess this was
all a front for a robbers' nest.

Jack chuckled to himself as he drew near the long,
low ranch house. Soon he would be part of the gang.
Unwittingly, they would help him satisfy his lifelong
desire to be rich.

In the ranch house, Bill Storey let his own armload of
wood clatter to the floor and dashed toward his angry
cousin. Turk Killam was backing away in fear as huge
Ernie Carpenter closed in.

Jumping in front of Ernie, Storey pressed stiff hands
against the giant's massive chest and said pleadingly,
"No, Ernie! Please! Don't do it!"

Respect for his cousin halted Ernie. He looked down
at Storey with his droopy eyes.

"You mustn't hurt Mr. Killam," Storey said, keeping
himself between Ernie and the bearded outlaw leader.

Ernie raised his eyes and looked past his cousin at a
frightened Turk Killam. There was an almost animal
contempt showing in Ernie's expression. "He was being
bad to Miss Lucy, Cousin Bill," came his slow reply.

"All . . . all I was doing," said Killam defensively,

"was asking her to go to the cellar and fetch me a bottle of whiskey."

Ernie swung his ponderous head around and looked at the lovely young woman. Stepping to her, he patted her shoulder gently and said, "I will go to the cellar for you, Miss Lucy." The boyish adoration he held for Lucy Daniels was apparent in his eyes.

Killam's anger surfaced, dispelling his fear. Bristling, he chopped the words with his teeth, "Look, Ernie, I'm the boss around here, and I give people their jobs. I didn't tell you to get the whiskey. I told Lucy to do it!"

Moving toward her stepfather, Lucy held her voice steady and said, "Turk, why make an issue out of nothing? Ernie has offered to get your bottle. Let him do it. He is happiest when he knows he is helping me."

Killam's black eyes hardened into icy marbles. Blowing smoke at her, he snapped, "The issue isn't *nothing*! The issue here is who is boss!"

Ernie headed for Killam, and Bill Storey leaped in front of him. "No, Ernie!" he gasped. "Mr. Killam isn't hurting Lucy!"

The muscles in Ernie's huge jaw flexed. "He blew smoke in her face. He yelled at her. That isn't nice. Move, Bill. I will make Mr. Turk sorry."

"Listen, Ernie," Storey said quickly, "Mr. Killam *is* sorry!"

The huge man sank the fingers of his left hand into the front of Storey's shirt, lifted him off the floor, and set him aside. "He never said he was sorry."

Dorothy Killam let out a tiny cry from her bed. She knew one blow from Ernie would kill her husband. Instantly, Lucy rushed to Ernie and laid a tiny hand on his massive, heaving chest. He froze in place, looking down at her tenderly.

"Mr. Killam really is sorry he blew smoke in my face and yelled at me," she blurted. Turning to her stepfather, she said, "Aren't you, Turk?"

Killam saw the danger in Ernie's eyes. "Uh . . . yeah." He nodded. "Yeah, I'm sorry."

Lucy gave Ernie careful instructions on where to find

the whiskey in the cellar and sent him on his way. The cellar door was just off the kitchen, near a large pantry.

When his heavy footsteps were heard descending the stairs, Killam's face crimsoned. He pointed a stiff finger at Storey and sprayed saliva as he growled, "Bill, I'm warning you! You'd better keep that muddle-brained monster in control, or else! You're a valuable man to me. But I will not be constantly threatened by a dumb idiot!"

Dorothy leaned up in her bed and said, "Turk, honey, if you'd be decent to Lucy, you would have no problem with Ernie."

Killam eyed her heavily for a moment and then looked at the big grandfather clock next to the fireplace. "Nearly five-thirty," he mumbled darkly. "If Bud ain't back here by six, yours truly is going to town after him."

Attempting to ease the tension in the room, Al Weems said, "Hey, Turk, are you really goin' to give Henry Yates five thousand in nuggets for feeding us the information?"

Killam threw his head back and laughed. "All that Yates is gonna get, Al, is hot lead. I sure ain't sharing none of my cut with the little weasel. And I doubt that any of you boys want to chip in five thousand. Seems to me there's only one thing we can do with Yates. Can't have him squawking, and dead men don't squawk."

Lucy looked at her stepfather with unbelieving eyes. Her full-curved lips pulled thin, and the steel pressure of her temper gave her cheeks a harsh, honed-down tautness. "Turk Killam," she scorned, "you are nothing but a cold-blooded killer! I don't know why you have to be a thieving outlaw in the first place. Henry Yates is just as much a thief as you are, and he deserves whatever the law might do to him. But he has helped you! This wicked thing couldn't even be done without him. Yet the thanks he gets from you is to be murdered?"

Killam's finger shook with fury as he blared heatedly, "I've had just about enough out of you, young lady! Now, you shut your trap, or I'm going to rearrange that pretty face of yours!"

Dorothy broke into sobs, begging her husband not to hurt Lucy. Ignoring her pleas, the stout-bodied man lashed out at the young woman again. "It's none of your business what I do, including who I kill. This gang has put a lot of men six feet under that you don't know anything about. Now you just butt out and tend to your mother."

Lucy stared back, cold and defiant. Through her teeth, she hissed, "You'll get yours someday."

Killam raised a hand to slap her, but checked it when he heard the sound of Ernie Carpenter returning from the cellar. Lowering his voice, he warned, "You just mind your own business, girl."

At the same moment, Hugh Pyle stuck his head in the door and said, "Hey, boss. There's a rider coming. Must be Hatch."

Killam stomped toward the door, saying, "He'd better have an almighty powerful excuse for being late!"

Lucy rubbed her mother's stiff body and salved the bedsores on her elbows while the gang gathered on the porch to meet Bud Hatch. Like an orphan puppy, big Ernie stayed at Lucy's heels.

As the rider drew closer, Bill Storey squinted and said, "Boss, that isn't Hatch's horse."

Hugh Pyle added, "That ain't Hatch, either."

Jack Taubert studied the cluster of men on the long, low-roofed porch by the light of the setting sun. Drawing near, he focused on their wary faces and the ominous black muzzles that were pointed his way.

Reining in some twenty feet from the porch, Jack saw two of the men leave the porch and circle around behind him, guns in hand.

Looking into the faces on the porch, the yellow-haired outlaw said, "I'm looking for Turk Killam."

"You found him," grunted the bearded one.

"My name is Jack Taubert. There was a shooting in El Paso at the Broken Horseshoe Saloon. Bud Hatch is dead."

Sudden shock was visibly stamped on Killam's florid face. He held the weight of his dark eyes on the slender man and said, "How'd it happen?"

"Got in a fight over a woman. I killed the jasper who plugged Bud."

Killam swung a fist through the air and swore. "Damn, he couldn't have picked a worse time!"

"You mean because of the Lone Star agent?" asked Jack with a sly grin.

Killam narrowed his eyes. "Just what do you know about it?"

"All of it." Jack let the word settle a few seconds before adding, "I mean the whole sixty-thousand-dollar ball of wax."

"All right, mister," demanded Killam, "who *are* you?"

"I told you—Jack Taubert. I am a—I *was* a friend of Bud's."

"From where?" asked Al Weems.

"Huntsville. We did time together."

The outlaws looked at each other. They knew Bud Hatch had told no one in town of his stretch in Huntsville prison. He was quite private about his prison record.

Jack saw them relax slightly. "Mind if I get out of this hard old saddle?" he asked Killam.

"Climb down."

Leather squeaked as the gaunt outlaw dismounted. Turning from the horse, he noticed the gang members holstering their weapons.

Stepping up to the edge of the porch as the two men behind him came in close, Taubert looked Killam in the eye and said, "Bud didn't die right away. He lived long enough to give me a message for you."

Arching his bushy eyebrows, Killam said, "And?"

"I'm supposed to tell you that Henry Yates says the full sixty-thousand-dollar shipment in gold nuggets is in the big vault at the Bank of El Paso. It is under guard twenty-four hours a day by three Pinkerton men."

"Sounds like Taubert, here, is telling us the truth,

boss," spoke up Dirk Holstead. "He wouldn't know any of this unless Bud had told him."

Killam pulled a fresh cigar out of his shirt pocket, bit off the end, and spit it on the ground. Striking a match on the seat of his pants, he raised the flame, cupping it against the breeze. Before touching fire to the tip, he asked, "What else did Bud tell you, Taubert?"

"Couple of things," came Jack's response. "One was that there's a Texas Ranger riding into El Paso on horseback from Austin. Only he's masquerading as a businessman from Las Cruces. This Ranger and the Pinkerton trio are going to nursemaid the gold to Austin in regular luggage on the stagecoach."

Bill Storey laughed heartily. "Bud told you that?"

"Yep." Jack nodded. "Said this is what Yates told him."

Storey pushed his hat to the back of his head and looked at Killam skeptically. "Turk," he said, "this doesn't make sense. We all know the Lone Star company ships gold in a wagon with an army escort. Why the sudden change? And why would they risk that fortune practically unprotected on a flimsy stagecoach? I'll tell you what it is. It's a trick, and this long-haired dude is in on it."

Jack Taubert looked at him with steady eyes, unflinching.

"It's a trick, I tell you, Turk," insisted Storey. "They'll have an army unit riding close by. The stagecoach will be bait. They'll draw us in with the bait. We start to hold up the stage, and the cavalry will move in and wipe us out."

"Now just hold on a minute, Bill," said Killam, waving his smoking cigar at him. "Hauling the gold like that *would* be a pretty good ruse. Who would expect they'd roll that fortune right past our noses? We would never know."

"Yeah," joined in Hugh Pyle. "And if some road agents just happened to hold up that particular stage, they'd be looking for whatever valuables were aboard to be in a strongbox. They'd never bother going through regular suitcases. Sounds pretty smart to me."

"I don't know," spoke up Al Weems. "I agree with Bill. Sounds like a sneaky setup."

"Well, it's something that'll bear checking into," said Killam, "but that don't mean that Taubert here is in on it. Seems to me he's got to be genuine. Why else would Bud trust him with all this information?"

"That adds up, boss," agreed Storey.

Looking at Jack Taubert, Killam said, "Let's go in the house and sit down before we go any further."

The outlaws filed inside. Jack Taubert noticed the invalid woman on the narrow, elevated bed.

"That's my missus," said Killam. "Dorothy," he called across the room, "this is Mr. Taubert."

"Howdy, ma'am." Jack grinned, exposing his yellow teeth.

Dorothy nodded wordlessly.

Through the kitchen door, Jack could see a young woman at the big iron cookstove. A huge man in bib overalls was helping her start a fire in the stove.

Calling toward the kitchen, Killam said, "Lucy! Put another plate on the table. We have a guest for supper." Swinging his face toward Jack, he said, "You *will* stay for supper?"

"Oh, yeah, sure." Jack smiled. "Much obliged."

The rough-looking men found seats in the big room. Killam turned to Jack. "Now what else did Bud tell you?"

Jack pulled out some papers and a pouch of tobacco from his shirt pocket and began rolling a cigarette. "Before he was shot, he told me that you were looking for a new man to take Dexter Wilson's place. Said Wilson got in the way of a bullet up in Santa Fe. He was going to bring me out here with him to see if you'd take me into the gang. I figure with Bud gone, too, you just might consider it."

Killam chewed on his cigar under the watchful eyes of the other gang members. Running his dark gaze over their faces, he looked back at Jack and said, "How long were you in Huntsville?"

"Three years."

"What for?"

"Armed robbery. Got out early for good behavior. I'm only bad when I'm on the *outside*. Behind the big gray walls, I'm a model citizen."

Laughter made the rounds.

"I assume you can handle that iron on your hip," said the outlaw leader.

"Ask the guy who shot Bud Hatch," quipped Jack. Then he snapped his fingers. "Whoops! Can't ask him. He's dead!"

The gang laughed again.

Running his gaze over the faces of the men again, Killam said, "Boys, there's no way Taubert could know all of this unless Bud had told him. Especially about Dex being killed at Santa Fe. I say if he was Bud's friend and Bud trusted him, he's welcome in this outfit. Any objections?"

At that moment, Lucy entered the room and immediately caught Jack Taubert's appreciative gaze. She turned a pair of thoroughly cool eyes on him.

"Lucy," called Killam, "this is Mr. Jack Taubert. Jack, that's my daughter, Lucy."

"*Stepdaughter*," she corrected him. Giving Jack a brief glance, she said, "Evening, Mr. Taubert."

"Ma'am." Jack grinned, hungrily following her movements as she walked to her mother's bed.

"Okay," Killam called after her with a false friendliness in his voice, "but you're the same as a daughter to me."

Everyone in the room except Jack Taubert knew it was a deliberate lie.

"How long till supper, Lucy?" Killam asked her.

"About an hour," came the reply.

"Good!" he exclaimed. "Then we can have a few nips before supper. Where's that bottle Ernie brought up from the cellar?"

"I think it's in the kitchen," answered Lucy. "Ask Ernie. He's in there."

Turk Killam's heavy voice filled the room as he bellowed, "Ernie! You in the kitchen?"

Jack turned and looked in amazement as the gigantic man ducked his head and moved through the door, setting his droopy, half-vacant eyes on Killam.

"What did you want, Mr. Turk?" Ernie asked in his slow, methodical manner.

"Where's the bottle I sent for?"

Ernie thought for a moment under Jack Taubert's examining eye. Jack had never seen a human being that big. He studied the towering height, the huge muscular arms, the thick, sloping shoulders, the ponderous, oversize head. The man was a mountain of strength.

Shaking his head, Ernie said, "Uh . . . the bottle is in the cupboard, Mr. Turk."

"Well, let's have it, son!" blared the bearded man.

Ernie turned slowly and reentered the kitchen.

"Lucy, dear," said Killam in a sweet tone that was totally foreign to his character, "would you be so kind as to bring us some glasses?"

The lovely brunette gave him a sour look and followed Ernie into the kitchen.

As the outlaws sipped their whiskey, Jack Taubert's eyes kept straying to Lucy, who had returned to her mother's bedside. The delectable aroma of food cooking was in the air.

"Now as I was saying, boys," said Killam, "I think we ought to take Taubert into the fold. Any of you have objections?"

To a man, the outlaws agreed that Jack ought to be welcomed in. Formal introductions were made all around.

"The boys will show you where to bunk after supper, Taubert," Killam said amiably. "Your horse gets free room and board. There's no salary for the work you'll do around the ranch. We all live off the jobs we pull. The ranch work is shared equal among the men."

Lucy walked back into the kitchen, and Killam saw Jack's eyes follow her. "Forget it," he told him.

Meeting Killam's gaze, Jack said, "Huh?"

"You make a move to lay a hand on her, Ernie will break your neck." Clearing his throat at the guilty look on Jack's face, Killam said, "We split all the money from the jobs forty-sixty. I take forty percent, you boys split the sixty among yourselves evenly. Sound okay?"

"Sure." Jack nodded.

"So you'll get a fifth of sixty percent when we take that sixty thousand in gold."

"Seventy-two hundred," Jack said a moment later.

Raising his eyebrows, Killam said, "Plenty fast with the figures, ain't you?"

Jack gave him a wolfish grin. "When it comes to money, Turk, there ain't nobody faster than Jack Taubert."

Killam laughed.

You wouldn't laugh, thought the yellow-haired outlaw, *if you knew that Jack Taubert is going to end up with one hundred percent of the gold!*

While consuming his portion of the whiskey, Killam said to Jack Taubert, "You told us you were in Huntsville prison with Bud, but where are you from?"

"San Antonio," responded Jack.

"So you were just drifting through El Paso and happened to run into Bud, I assume."

Jack tilted his head. "Not exactly drifting. I was going through on purpose. I have a younger brother who's working on a ranch due west of here a few miles. Place called the B-Bar-S."

Killam nodded. "Ben Sanders."

"Yeah. That's the name. Tommy mentioned it in his letter. I'll have to ride to the B-Bar-S in the morning. Little family business to handle. I'll leave at sunrise but should be back by early afternoon."

Killam nodded his assent and then pointed at Storey. "Bill is chore boss. He'll assign you work around here. Now let me go over the picture for you on this gold robbery."

Killam explained that they would have to keep close contact with Henry Yates. Their plans could not be finalized until the Texas Ranger arrived and gave Yates the time and details of the gold shipment.

"Once the gold is ours," Killam continued, "we're gonna stash it in a cave on the west side of the Franklins. The cave is well hidden and about fifty yards deep, with a five-foot-wide crevice opening. The crevice is fronted by a huge cluster of mesquite trees. You'd have to know it was there to ever find it. The gold will be safe there, and once the heat is off, we'll divide it up."

Bill Storey spoke up. "Boss, I'm still jittery about this stagecoach thing. I'm telling you, it's a setup."

Chewing on his cigar, Killam said, "You could be right, Bill, but I don't think so."

"But if Bill is right," put in Al Weems, "our goose is cooked."

"Just to be on the safe side, boss," said Hugh Pyle, "why don't we hit them when the gold is being transferred from the bank to the stagecoach? Yates will know when they're going to do it."

"Too risky," Killam said, shaking his head. "Bart Langford and his deputy will no doubt assemble an army of townsmen to stand guard. They'll do it at night, I'm sure, so no one will be around to see it."

Storey drained his glass. "Turk, I think we ought to stick with our original plan to go after the gold right where it is. We can figure a way to lure Marshal Langford and that deputy out of town. With them out of the way, we can handle the bank employees and those three Pinkerton boys."

The bearded outlaw leader blew a mouthful of smoke toward the beamed ceiling and sighed. "Sure would be a snap if this stagecoach thing is for real. We could waylay the stage a few miles east of town."

"It would be a big chance to take, boss," spoke up Dirk Holstead. "I think Bill and Al just might be right. Sure could be a trick. Besides, if *it is* for real, we'd probably have to kill the Ranger and those Pinkerton men. Maybe the driver and shotgunner, too."

"So what?" Hugh Pyle asked, fixing Holstead with a hard glare. "You queasy about killing?"

"Not queasy," objected Holstead. "I just don't see any sense in killing people if it can be avoided."

Turning to Killam, Pyle said, "Where'd you get this Sunday school boy, Turk?"

Leaping to his feet, Holstead stood over Pyle, who remained seated. Pyle eyed him coldly as the angry man said, "The more people we kill, the greater our chances of swinging at the end of a rope! Maybe you like the idea of hanging, but I don't."

Pyle held his icy eyes on Holstead. "Are you through?"

"No, I'm not!" lashed Holstead. "I've been with Turk for three years. If Turk has any complaints about me, he can voice them."

Pyle had a wicked eye and an evident mean streak. Inside, he wanted to retaliate at Holstead's outburst. He was not sure of his standing yet with Turk Killam, so he decided to let it pass. "You've had your say, Holstead," he said, tight lipped. "You can sit down now."

Jack Taubert liked Pyle. He had grit. He was cool, calculating, and would kill without remorse. It was in the man's icy blue eyes.

Killam watched Holstead burn Pyle with a hot glare and then return to his seat. "Dirk is all right, Hugh," he said with conviction. "He's dependable. Now, I want you boys to get along with each other."

Pyle responded with a tight, unreadable grin.

Turning to Storey, Killam said, "Bill, you ride into town in the morning and have a talk with Yates. If the stagecoach thing seems too shaky, we'll proceed with the original plan."

Storey was voicing his agreement when Lucy appeared at the kitchen door and told the men that supper would be ready shortly.

At the supper table, Jack Taubert found himself seated directly across from Ernie Carpenter, who sat next to Lucy. The huge man slurped his food hungrily, wolfing it down in large portions.

Jack had removed his hat. While chewing with his mouth open, Ernie appraised his long, stringy yellow hair for several minutes. Slowly, he ran his dull gaze between Lucy's shoulder-length hair and Jack's. Innocently, Ernie said to the skinny outlaw, "How come you don't wear a dress, lady?"

Lucy stifled a laugh, throwing her hand to her mouth.

Jack squirmed, his face tinting. Flustered, he eyed Ernie harshly and said, "I'm no lady. I'm a man."

Ernie swallowed his food, blinking in disbelief. "Then how come your hair is long like Miss Lucy's?"

Jack glared at him wordlessly.

The others around the table were suppressing their own laughter, when Killam's heavy voice broke the silence. "Lucy," he said, "when you and Ernie drive into town for groceries tomorrow, Bill is going along. He will tend to some business for me. He'll have his horse in case he has to stay awhile. I want you and Ernie to head for home just as soon as the wagon is loaded."

A frown touched the brunette's lovely brow. "But I promised Ernie he could watch the horse races for a while. You know how he loves animals. He has never seen horses race, and I think he would enjoy it."

"You heard me," Killam said in a half growl. "Just do like I say."

Standing abruptly, Lucy gave Killam a cold look. "I'll feed Mother now," she said with clipped words.

Later that evening when the dishes were done, Lucy was fluffing her mother's pillow. The men had vacated the house, leaving the two women alone. Lucy noticed tears in Dorothy's eyes. "What's wrong, Mother?" she asked tenderly.

Dorothy sniffed, her lower lip trembling. Biting down on her lip, she said, "Honey, I can't stand it anymore. Turk is getting meaner. He's like a wild beast. I can't bear to see the way he treats you. One of these days in a temper fit, he's going to hurt you seriously."

Lucy patted her mother's hand. "I'll be all right."

"No, honey," said Dorothy, rolling her head on the pillow, "you've got to leave this place. Tonight."

"Mother—"

"Listen to me, child," sniffed the invalid woman, "as soon as all the men are asleep, you saddle a horse and ride. Go to El Paso and get on a stagecoach to Laredo. Any of our old friends there would take you in. You can begin a new life for yourself—find a nice young man and get married."

Lucy's head was moving slowly back and forth. "No, darling," she said softly. "I will never leave you. I only wish there was a way to get *you* away from this awful place."

"I wouldn't leave if there were," Dorothy said through pallid lips. "You need to live your life without this crippled millstone hanging about your neck."

"Mother, you are not a—"

"Besides," cut in Dorothy, "I couldn't leave Turk. You know that."

Lucy Daniels knew it only too well. Her mother hated what Turk Killam had become and the way he treated Lucy, but she felt a heavy debt of gratitude toward the man.

Twelve years previously, Dorothy had been a destitute widow in Laredo, with an eleven-year-old daughter to raise. There was poor shelter, a meager supply of food, and no money. A legitimate rancher at the time, Killam had long had his eye on lovely Dorothy Daniels, enchanted with her beauty. He was ecstatic when her husband died. He watched and waited, and when Dorothy's plight became desperate, he went to her and offered marriage. She immediately saw an answer to her problems. The man was well off financially, and he would provide a home and security for herself and Lucy.

Though Dorothy made no pretense of being in love with Turk Killam, she accepted his proposal. They were married within a week. Two years later, the move was made to the present location.

Dorothy blamed herself for what Killam had become. He had been an honest, hard-working rancher until her accident six years ago. When he learned that she was paralyzed for life, something snapped inside him, and he grew hard and bitter. Though he was still tender toward his invalid wife, money became his passion. He became an outlaw, fronting his activities with the ranch.

Money was now more than plentiful in the Killam household, but the home had become unbearable. Especially for Lucy.

Dorothy was deeply disturbed over the kind of men her husband had brought onto the ranch. They were wicked, lewd men who would ravage her daughter but for their fear of Ernie Carpenter. Dorothy was in constant sorrow over Lucy's miserable state and evident unhappiness, but there was no way to alter the situation. She owed Killam a debt for taking her and Lucy in, and she meant what she had said. Even if she could, she would not leave him. The only possible answer to Lucy's plight was for her to forsake her mother and ride away.

The invalid woman looked deep into Lucy's dark blue eyes and saw what was clearly evident: Her devoted daughter would never leave as long as her mother was alive . . . no matter how much she suffered from Turk Killam's brutality.

Chapter Seven

A few miles west of the Killam ranch, the pale moon was spraying its silver light over the B-Bar-S ranch. Young Tommy Taubert was strolling along the bank of a meandering brook with lovely Melinda Sanders, daughter of the wealthy owner of the ranch.

Standing an even six feet in height, twenty-year-old Tommy was a handsome, one-hundred-and-sixty-five-pound cowboy. He had neatly trimmed, ash-blond hair, medium-length sideburns, and an angular, suntanned, clean-shaven face. Tommy's amiable personality was enhanced by the warm, ready smile on his lips and the convivial sparkle in his sky-blue eyes.

Melinda held Tommy's arm as they walked slowly, listening to the music of the brook. After some time, he stopped and kicked a fist-sized rock into the water. "I don't think I can stand it, Melinda," he said, turning to her.

Melinda tilted her face up toward the tall cowboy and did not try to mask the concern that etched her delicate features. "Tommy, I won't let Lloyd so much as hold my hand. I promise. You are the one I love."

"Stinking races," he said disgustedly. "Why do they have to have them right now?"

She touched his face. "If it weren't the races, darling, it would be something else. Daddy insists that I see Lloyd on occasion."

"Does he really think he can make you fall in love with that fellow?"

"He knows he can't force it." She sighed. "But he

thinks if we are together enough, it will just happen. But it can't ever happen. I'm in love with you, Tommy."

The lanky cowboy looked down at the petite woman. He loved her for everything she was. What Melinda Sanders lacked in size, the vivacious beauty made up in tenderness and congeniality. He let his eyes drink in her long, lovely hair. Even in the moonlight, it resembled spun gold. Then he stared into her large brown eyes, which were exquisitely set in an expressive, finely formed face.

"Just give it time, darling," she said softly. "You know my father. He is hardheaded and stubborn. When he gets his mind set on something, he is tenacious. Mother says I am just like him in that category. My mind is set on becoming Mrs. Tommy Taubert, so I will have to be even *more* tenacious. If I don't make him give up this Lloyd Candler idea by the time I turn twenty-one, I will marry you in spite of Daddy."

"That's a year and a half away," groaned the young man. "I've been hoping we could get married when *I* turn twenty-one."

"Don't give up on the idea," she said, pulling her lips into a smile. "That's four months away. A lot can happen in four months."

Tommy put the tips of his fingers under Melinda's graceful chin, tilting her lips toward his own. "Okay, Miss Optimism." He grinned. "I'll tolerate Candler a little longer—although I wish he would fall and break his neck on the way over here tomorrow."

"Why, Mr. Taubert," she said with a tiny giggle, "you are a vicious man!"

Folding her into his arms, he said, "When it comes to someone else even *thinking* you could be interested in him, you are right. I am a vicious man."

Their lips came together in a warm, lingering kiss.

Looking into her eyes once again, he said in a half whisper, "I love you, Melinda."

"And I love you, Tommy," she replied, kissing him again. "Now we'd best be getting back to the house."

Twenty minutes later, a pair of stern eyes watched from an upstairs window as the young couple strolled into the yard.

The early morning sun cast its slanted rays through the kitchen windows as Melinda entered the room, drawn by the aroma of hot food.

"Good morning, Martha," chirped Melinda to the buxom, middle-aged cook.

The large woman warmed the rancher's daughter with a smile. "Good mornin', honey. You look happy today. I'll bet it's because you're goin' to the horse races with that handsome Candler boy!"

Melinda's eyes dulled. "He's not so handsome," she said dryly.

At that moment, Evelyn Sanders appeared. Martha shook her head in puzzlement at Melinda's remark as Evelyn said, "Well, how is my favorite daughter this morning?"

"Fine, Mother." Melinda smiled, kissing her cheek.

Turning to Martha, Evelyn said, "And how is my favorite cook?"

"Just fine," replied Martha.

A tall, slender man with a thick head of silver hair entered the room. "Well, here they are," he said exuberantly, "the three women in my life!" Pecking each one on the cheek, Ben Sanders took his seat at the breakfast table and plunged in like a hungry bear. His very presence dominated the room. The wealthy rancher was king in his castle, and everybody knew it.

As the meal progressed, Evelyn kept her husband talking about anything and everything, attempting to delay the inevitable as long as possible. When she ran out of subjects, Sanders looked at his daughter, who sat directly across from him, and said, "Melinda, we need to have a little talk."

Evelyn pushed her chair back, saying, "I've got some sewing to do."

Touching her arm gently, the rancher said, "No, dear, I would like you to be in on this."

Evelyn, who was twelve years younger than her sixty-year-old husband and a lovely older version of her daughter, eased back into place.

Picking up a cup of black coffee, Ben Sanders looked at his daughter through the steam and said, "Melinda, this is not to upset you, honey, but I am becoming concerned about the relationship you are allowing to develop between yourself and Tommy."

Melinda looked at him with hurt in her eyes and said acridly, "You mean Tommy and I can't be friends?"

"I think it's getting beyond that," responded her father. "I know what lovelight looks like, and it is becoming evident in his eyes when he looks at you."

"But Daddy, you—"

"Moonlight walks are an indication of a relationship getting serious, Melinda. You mustn't lead this young man on. He—"

"Daddy," cut in the golden-haired woman, "what have you got against Tommy?"

"Absolutely nothing as a cowhand," came the rancher's instant reply. "But everything as a potential son-in-law."

With pain in her voice, Melinda said, "I've heard you say many times that Tommy is the best worker on the ranch."

Placing his coffee cup in its saucer, Sanders nodded. "He is, without a doubt. He sets a good example for the other men and encourages them to work efficiently. I like Tommy. He is honest, straightforward, and as clean-cut as they come. In fact, even though he's the youngest of the bunch, I'm leaning strongly toward making him B-Bar-S foreman when old Charlie Thomas retires next year."

"Then why do you object to Tommy and me being interested in each other?"

Sanders took a deep breath, glanced at his wife, and said, "Melinda, do I really have to spell it out for you?

Tommy Taubert is a mere ranch hand. You and he are not on the same social level. Lloyd Candler is the son of a man of financial means. Wyman Candler's family is good stock—the kind that I would like my grandchildren to come from."

Whiteness showed on Melinda's cheeks, making the dark brown of her eyes more prominent. "Tommy will not always be a *mere* ranch hand, as you put it," she said through lips that scarcely moved. "I heard you tell Mother several weeks ago that he has a good business head on him."

Evelyn Sanders nervously adjusted her position on the chair as she felt the weight of Melinda's eyes on her. Looking at her husband, she said, "You did say, Ben, that Tommy had done extremely well to save enough money on cowboy's wages to buy that Texas longhorn heifer from you. And I remember how pleased you were when he used that inheritance money to build his herd. How many longhorns does he own now?"

"I think he has a dozen head," replied the rancher. "Within ten or twelve years, he will no doubt be ranching on his own."

"He won't be *a mere* ranch hand then, will he?" pressed Melinda.

"Well, if we're talking about you and Tommy being married," growled Sanders, "you would be thirty years old. Is that what you want? You want to be an old maid while he's waiting for his stock to multiply?"

Melinda's lips drew into a thin, clamped line. "What would be wrong in my marrying a man with potential and standing by him and helping him reach his goal of being a successful rancher?"

A bit flustered, Sanders said, "But what if something happened and he didn't make it? There is that risk, you know. With Lloyd Candler there is no risk. Wyman told me that when Lloyd gets married, he is going to give him a ranch of his own—set him up with plenty of land, brand-new house and buildings, and several thousand head of cattle."

"Tommy *will* make it, Daddy," she replied. "But even if he didn't, I would stay by him."

"Melinda," said the rancher with sand in his voice, "we don't know anything about Tommy's family. I want my grandchildren to have pedigree. Now, we've discussed this long enough. You are to break off this relationship with Tommy immediately. And what's more, you are to warm up to Lloyd. I've noticed you being a little cool to him lately. He has asked me privately for permission to court you. I gave him my consent."

The petite young woman shoved her chair back and stood up. Her lovely features snapped with anger. Her eyes bored into his like sharp-pointed augers. "Lloyd Candler may have your permission to court me," she rasped, "but he does not have *mine!*"

Later that morning, the housekeeper, Martha, responded to a knock at the front door of the large two-story house.

"Good morning, ma'am," said the skinny, yellow-haired visitor, lifting his hat. "I couldn't raise nobody over the bunkhouse, so I thought I'd check here. I'm looking for Tommy Taubert."

Martha eyed the greasy, stringy hair that hung limply on Jack Taubert's narrow shoulders. The odor from his body invaded her nostrils. Backing up a step and eyeing him with disdain, she said, "He's out on the range somewhere. Won't be in till sundown."

"I can't wait that long, ma'am," said Jack. "Is there anyone around who could tell me how to find him?"

"Just a moment," she said. "Wait here."

Ben Sanders looked up from the desk where he sat in the den, as Martha tapped on the doorjamb. "What is it, Martha?"

"Mr. Sanders," she said softly, "there's a man out on the front porch who says he's looking for Tommy Taubert. Even looks something like him. Wants to know where Tommy is out on the range so he can go find him."

Standing up, the rancher moved toward her, saying, "I'll talk to him."

As he passed her, Martha said, "Mr. Sanders . . ."

"Yes?"

"Don't get downwind of him."

Sanders shook his head, not being sure he heard the woman correctly. Reaching the front door, he took one look at the wiry man and understood her warning. Over the man's shoulder, Ben saw his wife and daughter approaching the porch in the brilliant sunlight.

"I understand you're looking for Tommy," Sanders said in a level tone.

"Yes, sir. I'm his brother, Jack. Just rode in from San Antonio. Have a little family business to tend to, and I need to see Tommy right away."

At that instant, Evelyn and Melinda topped the steps and moved across the broad porch to the door. Jack was blocking their way. Evelyn cleared her throat.

The skinny man whipped his hatless head around. "Oh, excuse me, ladies." He chuckled, stepping aside.

Mother and daughter stepped past him, both getting a sufficient whiff. They moved quickly to the parlor, looking at each other in amazement. Out of earshot, they both whispered at once, "He looks like Tommy!"

Easing back toward the vestibule, they listened as Sanders gave the stranger directions on where to find Tommy out on the range. When Jack walked away, the women met Sanders as he turned from the door. The rancher's face was rigid.

"Who was he?" queried Evelyn.

"Tommy Taubert's brother," he replied, setting his gaze on Melinda. "What was I saying at breakfast about pedigree?"

The golden-haired young woman was dumbfounded.

"Tommy's been with us for over two years, now," spoke up Evelyn. "He told us about his parents being dead, but he has never mentioned having a brother."

Sanders stepped back to the door and set his eyes on Jack Taubert, who was now a hundred yards away, riding fast. The two women joined him, also eyeing the diminishing figures of horse and rider.

The rancher waited a long moment and then looked down at Melinda, his brow furrowed. With a jagged edge to his voice, he said, "I wonder what else Tommy has not told us."

The heat of the sun bore down on the five B-Bar-S men as they knelt around the longhorn cow that lay prostrate on the ground. One of the men held her head twisted back while Tommy Taubert applied salve to her bruised and bleeding udder. The frightened animal's eyes were bulging, and she was breathing heavily.

Finishing the application, Tommy said, "Okay, Bob, let her up."

The cow hoisted herself onto all fours with a grunt, swished her tail at the cowhands, and trotted off to join several dozen cattle that were clustered thirty yards away.

Young Taubert was squeezing the lid onto the can of salve when one of the hands said, "Somebody's coming."

Tommy glanced at the rider who was approaching at a gallop and then placed the can in his saddlebag. Pulling a large bandanna from his hip pocket, he mopped sweat from his face and neck.

He heard another one of the hands say, "It ain't a B-Bar-S man."

While stuffing the bandanna back in his pocket, Tommy eyed the rider again. A slight gasp escaped from his lips. He squinted, making sure he was seeing correctly.

"What is it, Tommy?" asked one.

"Well, I'll be a—" The lanky cowboy ran forward a few yards, waving at the rider, who ejected a war whoop, waving back.

Within seconds, the scrawny rider skidded to a halt and bounded from the saddle.

"Jack!" hollered the younger brother.

"Howdy, Tommy!" laughed the older one as they embraced and danced each other in a circle.

They stopped, and Jack stepped back, his palms on his taller brother's shoulders. "Hey, look at you!" he exclaimed. "You're not my *little* brother anymore!" Cuffing his jaw playfully, he said, "But I can still whip you!"

"Don't count on that," chortled Tommy, cuffing him back. Turning to the cowboys, who stood in amusement, he said, "Hey, fellas! I want you to meet my brother!"

"Didn't know you had one, Tommy," one of them said as they closed in.

Introductions were made, and then young Taubert said, "Why don't you boys ride on over to that next draw? I'll chat with Jack for a few minutes and catch up, okay?"

The men agreed and rode away.

Turning to his brother, Tommy said, "I was a little stunned when I got your letter that you were out of prison, Jack. Your sentence wasn't up for nearly two years." His face clouded. "You didn't—"

"Break out?" Jack laughed. "Now, c'mon, kid. You fret too much. I didn't escape. I got paroled. Time off for good behavior. Why, when the warden unlocked the gate to let me out, he bowed and said, 'You've been a model prisoner, Mr. Taubert, but please don't come back!' "

Tommy's sky-blue eyes showed his skepticism. He wanted to believe his brother, but little needles of doubt pricked at the back of his mind. Eyeing him warily, he said, "Jack, are you telling me the truth?"

The older Taubert raised his right hand and said solemnly, "The truth, kid. On Ma's grave. Pa's, too, if you like."

Tommy studied him cautiously.

Grinning, Jack said, "I'm just sorry it has taken us over a year to get together since I got out. How come it took you so long to send the letter telling me where you'd settled?"

Tommy explained that for the first year and a half

that he had been at the B-Bar-S, he kept expecting to pull up stakes and move on. It wasn't till about eight months ago that he had fallen in love with the enchanting desert and had decided to stay. Once that was settled, he had sent the letter. Since then, he had used his half of the inheritance to invest in Texas longhorn cattle.

When the inheritance was mentioned, Jack's face lit up. Rubbing his hands together, he said, "I can't wait to get hold of my half, kid. Where is it?"

Tommy Taubert saw the sudden naked greed in his brother's eyes. It was the same look of avarice that had been there years before. It was Jack's driving passion to be rich that had put him behind bars. A cold hand of disappointment clutched Tommy's heart. He had hoped that the prison sentence had changed him.

Setting his jaw, Tommy said, "Pa put a stipulation in the will, Jack. You are not to receive your half of the inheritance until you have worked an honest job for two years."

Jack looked at his brother in disbelief. "*Two years?*" he blurted, eyes bulging. "You're . . . you're not going to hold to it, are you? I need that money!"

"I have to honor Pa's request," Tommy said doggedly.

"Look, kid," breathed the older brother, "what do you think I've been doing since I got out of prison? I was working for the railroad east of San Antonio."

Jack was lying, but there was no way Tommy could verify it. He had actually lived by pulling small robberies and committing petty thefts.

"Good!" The younger Taubert grinned, eager to believe his brother. "Then if you get another good job and stick with it for a year, you can have your half of the inheritance."

A red flush went across Jack's hard features. "Now look, kid," he said, his breath hot, "this is ridiculous. That money isn't doing me no good sitting wherever you have it stashed. A parole for good behavior and a year of walking straight ought to be enough to please the old man."

Tommy bristled. "I never did like you calling Pa the *old man*, Jack. Wasn't what you did bad enough? You shamed the Taubert name and broke Ma and Pa's hearts. Now, I'll count the first year with the railroad. But you've got a year to go."

There was a quickening in Jack's pulse and a sudden hardening of his face muscles. "Why didn't you tell me in your letter about the two-year stipulation?" he demanded.

Tommy's eyes misted. "Because I wanted you close to me so I could help you walk straight. You're my brother, Jack. More than anything, I want you to be a decent citizen. I don't want any more black marks on the Taubert name."

Flustered, the outlaw brother stuck his hands in his hip pockets, turned his back to Tommy, and walked away, swearing under his breath. He went about forty feet, pivoted, and walked back stiff legged. Stopping only inches from Tommy, he regarded him coldly, his eyes like the dead of winter. Through clenched teeth, he said, "I want my money, kid."

Tommy's expression settled into an impassive mold. In a level tone, he said, "You'll get it when you do what Pa wrote in the will."

Jack's temper flared as raw fury soared through his brain. Money was his god. Nobody tampered with Jack Taubert's money. His sharp-edged features flushed red as his fist lashed out, punching Tommy square on the jaw.

Tommy felt his feet touch air, then his back slammed the ground. His vision blurred momentarily as the fuzzy form of his brother loomed over him.

"There's more where that came from!" Jack hissed. "Now you're gonna be reasonable about this thing, or else!"

Slowly, the younger brother rose to his feet, rubbing his jaw. "Don't do that again, Jack," he warned. "I don't want to fight you. Pa trusted me to handle the money, and I'm going to do it."

The veins in Jack's face distended, making him look

ugly and hostile. His eyes puckered in anger, and the muscles in his jaw knotted convulsively. "Looks like I'm gonna have to change your mind," he rasped. Again Jack's fist lashed out. Tommy saw it coming, and he ducked, causing Jack to miss.

"Stop it! Don't make me fight you!" Tommy pleaded.

"I want my money!" snarled the older brother, swinging wildly.

Tommy bobbed away from the punch and launched one of his own. He caught Jack solidly on the nose and sent him rolling. Jack got up, shaking his head, blood bubbling in his nose. When he saw the blood, he roared like a wild beast and charged, both fists pumping.

The younger Taubert sent a hissing punch to the hollow of Jack's jaw and followed it with two more quick blows. Jack went down again.

"Now that's enough!" Tommy shouted, as his bloody brother rose to his feet again.

"It ain't enough till I have my money," Jack said coldly, sniffing blood. With that, he charged again, fists swinging.

This time Tommy planted his feet and put his weight behind a violent punch to Jack's temple. The yellow-haired outlaw went down in a heap, rolled in the dust, and lay still. He was out cold.

Standing over him, Tommy fought the tears that welled up in his eyes. "Why, Jack?" he said to the unmoving form. "Why do you have to be like that? I didn't want to fight you. You're my brother."

Thumbing away the tears, Tommy went to his horse and took the canvas-wrapped canteen from the saddle. Returning to Jack, he poured water on his face.

The beaten man came to, rolling his head and moaning. Tommy helped him sit up. "I'm sorry, Jack," he said. "You made me do it."

Jack wiped the water from his face and replied, "Hey, kid, I'm the one that's sorry. Where'd you learn to fight like that?"

"Sort of picked it up along the way."

Slowly, the older brother gained his feet and checked

his nose. There was still a trickle of blood. Pulling out a dirty bandanna, he held it to his nose and began brushing himself off. The fire had gone from his eyes, and suddenly he seemed like a different person.

"I really am sorry, kid," Jack said through the bandanna. "I just lost my temper."

The crafty outlaw had quickly learned that he was not going to get his hands on the inheritance money by force. So he would try the soft approach. "I won't ever swing at you again," he assured his younger brother. "It's just that I've sort of been down on my luck. I'm out of funds. It seemed reasonable to me that a year on the railroad would be enough."

"Pa was only trying to bend you in the right direction by his stipulation," said Tommy.

"Yeah." Jack nodded, stooping to retrieve his dusty hat, "I know he was."

Tommy's gaze settled on the hair dangling on his brother's shoulders. "Is that why your hair is so long?" he asked. "Because you didn't have the money for a haircut?"

"Uh . . . yeah, kid," lied Jack. "I've been broke for quite a spell. Ever since I quit the railroad."

"There are plenty of ranches around these parts," said Tommy. "Wouldn't take you long to find a job. I'll give you a few dollars to tide you by."

Suddenly Jack remembered his deal with Turk Killam. Even though he was only staying long enough to see the robbery through and take the gold from Killam, he did have a job on the Killam ranch.

"Listen, kid," Jack said in a serious tone, "what if you found out that I already have been hired as a ranch hand. I mean, that it was *already* done. Would that convince you I mean to go straight?"

Tommy eyed him closely, hope rising in his breast. "Sure would."

"Well, that's exactly what I've done."

A slow grin worked its way over Tommy's handsome face. "Are you telling me the truth?"

"Tell you what," said the older brother, wiping a palm across his mouth, "if I take you to the rancher who just hired me yesterday, would you believe me? I mean, if he confirms it?"

"Well, of course!" responded Tommy, the spark of hope within him bursting into flame.

"Okay, I'll take you there right now. His name is Turk Killam."

"I know where the ranch is," said Tommy, now elated. "I pass it every time I go into El Paso."

"That's the place, kid!"

"And you've already been hired?"

"Yeah. Come on, let's ride over there, and you can ask Killam yourself."

"That's not necessary," Tommy said, his eyes filming with moisture. "I'll take your word for it. I only wish Ma and Pa could know."

"Maybe somehow they do, kid," said Jack tenderly, playing his part to the hilt.

Tommy sniffed, wiping tears with the back of his hand. His desire to see Jack forsake the life of an outlaw was so strong that he swallowed the act without question.

"Hey, kid," Jack continued, "would my getting the job without you pushing me into it maybe cause you to consider bending Pa's rule a little bit? I mean, with a year already with the railroad and all?"

Tommy was so overwhelmed with joy that he dropped all his defenses and said, "Sure, Jack. Sure."

"Where have you got the money?" asked Jack, disguising his excitement.

"It's in the Bank of El Paso," came the younger brother's answer. "I've got to get back to work now, but if you will come around at sundown and meet me at the bunkhouse, I'll write you a bank draft."

Tommy threw a glance in the direction of his coworkers. "I guess they can get along without me for a while. Okay, let's go."

As the ranch buildings came into view, Jack adjusted

himself in the saddle and said, "You know what would really be good, kid?"

"What's that?" asked Tommy.

"If you would ride into town with me. I'd cash the draft at the bank and then we could spend a little time together. After all, we've been apart for a long stretch."

Tommy Taubert was so pleased at the change in his brother that he would do anything to encourage him. "All right." He grinned. "I'll ask Mr. Sanders for the rest of the day off."

It took but moments for young Taubert to stop at the bunkhouse and write the one-thousand-dollar bank draft to his brother. Jack worked hard to conceal his pleasure as he folded it and placed it in a shirt pocket along with a pencil stub he always carried. Buttoning the pocket, he said, "Okay, kid, I'm set."

As the Taubert brothers rode toward the huge house, Tommy saw Lloyd Candler swinging from his saddle at the front porch. Ben Sanders emerged from inside and shook hands with Lloyd. One of the Sanders ranch hands had harnessed horses to the family surrey and was pulling it to a halt in front of the house.

Jack stayed in the saddle as Tommy dismounted and strode toward the rancher. Ben Sanders gave him a tight smile, saying, "Hello, Tommy."

The Sanders women came through the door, and Melinda's face lit up upon seeing the lanky cowboy. Tommy quickly explained the situation and asked for the rest of the day off. Sanders granted permission and then said, "I don't recall your mentioning that you had a brother."

"Guess there never was a reason to," he said, hunching his shoulders. "Thanks for the favor."

As young Taubert turned, he smiled at Melinda and then set his eyes on Lloyd Candler.

The wealthy rancher's son held a smug look on his face. "Going into town, cowboy?" he asked.

"Yeah." Tommy nodded.

"Maybe Melinda and I will see you at the races," Lloyd said with a facade of friendliness.

"Maybe." Tommy nodded without expression. Giving Melinda another smile, he mounted. "Thank you again, Mr. Sanders," he said from the saddle. Staring at Lloyd Candler with smoldering eyes, he rode away with his brother.

Chapter Eight

Vic Barry dismounted at the green oasis on the western edge of the salt flats and stared down at the sprawled forms of his two friends. The gunfighter swore vehemently. He ran his gaze to the pair of dead horses and then swore again. Stepping close to the bodies of the men, he saw buzzing green-backed flies feasting on the bullet wounds.

Lefty Muldane had died with his mouth and eyes wide open. Huge red ants were scurrying across the sightless eyes and crawling in and out of the mouth.

The scene spoke for itself. Someone had gunned down his two partners and got his own horse plugged in the shoot-out. Careful investigation of the area revealed that the killer had been alone. He had switched saddles and gone toward El Paso on Herb Nolan's blue roan.

Vic Barry spit tobacco in the hot sand and swung into the saddle. Squinting toward the vague outline of the jagged Franklin Mountains in the distance, he said aloud, "With that blue roan, the dude won't be hard to find. Sure hope he is enjoying the ride. It'll be his last one. He's already a dead man."

The hot wind was gusting and whipping up dust as Ernie Carpenter guided the wagon into El Paso and headed up San Francisco Street. Lucy Daniels rode beside her self-appointed bodyguard, firmly holding the brim of her large hat against the stubborn wind. Bill Storey trotted behind on his horse.

The colorful canvas banners that were suspended over the street popped and danced in the gusts. It was just after nine o'clock. The races would not begin until noon, but already El Paso's streets were bustling with people.

Ernie pulled the wagon to a halt in front of Hanson's General Store. Storey told Lucy and Ernie that he would see them later and then rode on toward the Lone Star Stagecoach office.

A half-dozen rowdies, ranging in age from seventeen to twenty, were loitering in front of the store, laughing boisterously while passing around a whiskey bottle. Ernie slowly lumbered to the ground from the wagon seat, drawing their attention immediately. They began pointing, snickering, and elbowing each other.

While the huge man rounded the wagon in his hulking manner, intending to help Lucy down, she looked across the street at the Bank of El Paso. The shades were still drawn on the windows. Lucy thought of the coveted gold inside the stone building. She was tempted to hasten to Marshal Bart Langford's office and tell him of Turk Killam's plans. Every fiber of her being wanted to do it, but fear clawed at her heart. If something went wrong and Killam was not caught, he would know who had told the marshal. Lucy knew that in his blind fury, Killam might kill her—and there would be no one to care for her mother.

The beautiful brunette could take Killam's wrath on herself but would do nothing to cause her invalid mother to suffer.

Lucy became aware of the snide comments of the rowdies as Ernie tied the horses to a hitching post and shuffled to her side of the wagon. She knew that he was aware of their taunts, but he ignored them. Lucy's heart went out to him. There was a real tenderness in his dull, drooping eyes. Often she looked at him and thought of a big, lovable St. Bernard. Left alone, the powerful giant would never harm anyone. Ordinarily, he took abuse toward himself in stride.

The big retarded man was intelligent enough to know

that he was far beneath those around him in intellect. It was his lot in life, and it did not embitter him. He only asked to be allowed to serve and protect Lucy Daniels. The only other objects of his care were the helpless creatures of the animal world.

Ernie was about to lift his hands up toward Lucy, when one of the boisterous young men shouted, "Hey, fellas, they forgot to harness the donkey in the bib overalls!"

Hoarse laughter made the rounds. An elderly couple passed by on the boardwalk, taking note of Ernie and the taunting. The old gentleman reprimanded them, saying, "You boys shouldn't tease him. Can't you see he is not all there?"

One of the teens guffawed and yelled, "If he ain't all there, Pop, where's the rest of him?"

Lucy's face suddenly flushed with anger. Standing up in the wagon, she pointed a finger at them. "You insolent hoodlums! Can't you find anything else to do? Shut your mouths! Don't you say another word about him!"

Ernie looked up at her with his sad eyes and said, "It's all right, Miss Lucy. I'm used to being laughed at. People like to make fun of me. I'm big and ugly and dumb."

The rowdies began whistling and making catcalls.

"Hey, boys!" laughed a two-hundred-pound young man who seemed to be their leader. "The cute little lady has a temper!"

"Yeah, Bo," snickered one with carrot-red hair as he waved the whiskey bottle. "She gets mad when we talk about her boyfriend!" More laughter followed.

Ernie looked at them and blinked. He knew something was different, but his brain had not quite picked up the fact that now Lucy was being insulted. Hoisting his hands to lift her down, he said, "Come on, Miss Lucy. Let's go in the store."

Lucy scorned the hecklers with blazing eyes as Ernie lowered her to the ground as if she weighed no more than a feather. The couple stepped up on the boardwalk.

Suddenly, the big one named Bo leaped in front of

them, blocking their way. The others quickly joined him.

"If I were you," Lucy said to Bo, "I would take my little friends and find somewhere else to play. Believe me, you don't want to get him mad."

Bo had big buck teeth, which caused his upper lip to protrude. "Ha!" he mocked. "That big lummox is so slow, I could punch him a dozen times before he could lift a hand to protect his mud-ugly puss!"

"You will please move now," Ernie said in his slow, thick-tongued manner. "Miss Lucy and I are going into the store."

The redhead handed the whiskey bottle to one of the others and stepped forward, pushing his face close to Lucy's. Ernie bristled.

"How about a big kiss for old Red, sweetie?" said the redhead, breathing whiskey fumes in her face.

Ernie's neck flushed, the crimson flow working steadily upward into his stiffening features.

"I *dare* you, Red!" blustered Bo, cocksure they were in control of the situation.

Abruptly, Red cupped the brunette's cheeks in his hands and planted a slobbery wet kiss on her lips. Lucy ejected a gagging sound and broke free.

Rage welled up in Ernie Carpenter. While it swelled and grew, the huge man ushered Lucy to the door of the general store, telling her to go inside. She started in and then wheeled to watch, wiping the bitter taste of the redhead's mouth from her lips.

Ernie turned around slowly, setting his sluggish gaze on Red. "You put your dirty mouth on Miss Lucy, mister," he said, shuffling toward him. "Now I will hurt you."

Turning to Bo, who now held the whiskey, Red snapped, "Gimme the bottle!" Seizing it, he smashed the bottom against a nearby hitch rail, leaving sharp, jagged edges protruding dangerously.

Lucy's hand flew to her mouth.

Ernie's face was now a shapeless crimson blur of fury. The redhead, egged on by his companions, leaped forward, swinging the deadly glass weapon. When it whistled past Ernie's nose, his huge meaty fist flashed out with amazing speed and seized Red's wrist.

The giant's grip was like a steel vise. Angrily he bore down. The broken bottle fell to the boardwalk, shattering into tiny pieces. Red howled as bone snapped in his wrist, and he fell to the boardwalk in agony.

"Let's get him, boys!" hollered big Bo.

Ernie had not yet released Red's wrist when Bo drove a pile-driving blow to his jaw. Ernie blinked, but showed no effect. Bo's eyes bulged in shock as he rubbed his fist. Suddenly, the other four youths leaped on Ernie, attempting to wrestle him to the ground. Lucy and the growing crowd of spectators watched in awe as the huge, slow-minded man stood erect, bearing the full weight of all four. They could not budge him.

Suddenly, Ernie unleashed his massive arms in a maelstrom of mindless fury. Four flailing bodies sailed through the air, landing hard on dirt and boardwalk.

Bo stepped in and swung a haymaker. His fist cracked as bone met bone. Ernie brushed at the spot on his jaw like a man would brush at a pesky fly. The vast strength that was locked up in his burly frame came loose in a violent, piston-style punch that landed square on Bo's heavy, protruding upper lip. The two hundred pounder sailed a dozen feet into the dusty street, arms and legs windmilling. He landed hard, unconscious, gagging on the teeth that were falling down his throat. His upper lip was spurting blood.

Ernie's anger was not abated. The redhead had dared to touch Lucy.

Red had scrambled to his feet and stood in the street holding his broken wrist. The other four had composed themselves and were gathered around him. When they saw Ernie coming, they scattered in fear, leaving Red standing alone.

Red stumbled, attempting to retreat, as Ernie closed in. Bending down, Ernie lifted the young man like a child would pick up a rag doll. In a flash, the giant had him locked face-to-face in a bear hug.

Red ejected a blood-curdling scream as the powerful arms bore down. Suddenly Lucy appeared beside Ernie, saying loudly, "No, Ernie! No! Let go of him! You'll kill him! Please, Ernie, let go!"

Ernie looked down at the beautiful young woman and let a smile curve his heavy lips. "All right, Miss Lucy," he said, dropping Red in a heap.

Taking him by the hand, she said, "Come on, Ernie, let's get what we came for and go home."

The hot, gusting wind plucked at Ranger Branson Howard's hat as he stepped out on the porch of the Rio Grande Hotel. The new iron-gray suit he wore enhanced his good looks. Though he usually wore his Colt on his hips, it was now riding higher. Businessmen wore guns for protection, but not low on their hips for a fast draw.

The dark-haired Ranger glanced up and down the street. It was alive with people. Forty yards to his right, Branson saw customers lining up for the ten o'clock opening of the bank. The door came open, and they began filing in.

Branson's attention was then drawn to a shuffle-footed giant of a man who was carrying boxes from the general store and loading them in a wagon. His attention then shifted as a lovely dark-haired woman emerged from the store and stood by the wagon. She held the brim of her hat to keep the gusting wind from stealing it away.

Nonchalantly, Branson strolled among the crowd, heading toward the wagon, eager to get a closer look at the beautiful woman. The big, slow-moving man came and went from the store, placing more boxes into the bed of the wagon.

Whirling dust devils skipped along the wagon-rutted street as the Ranger drew near the spot where the breathtaking brunette was standing. He paused thirty feet away, admiring the woman's beauty. The big man was easing a sack of flour into the wagon bed, saying,

"Only three more sacks, Miss Lucy, and we can go home."

As Lucy smiled at the big man, she unwittingly relaxed her grip on the hat. Suddenly, a gust of wind plucked the hat from her fingers. "Oh!" she exclaimed. "Ernie! My hat!"

Ernie lifted his huge head. His dull eyes followed the hat as it sailed across the street. His big, clumsy body moved into motion, lumbering toward the hat. The wind picked it up, carrying it farther.

Branson observed the scene, realizing that the big man might never catch the elusive hat. Quickly, he dashed past Ernie and retrieved it. The man looked at him with puzzled, half-empty eyes and followed as Branson carried it to Lucy. He gave Branson an unwholesome look. The curve of his mouth was sad and dispirited.

"Here's your hat, ma'am," Branson said.

"Thank you," Lucy replied, a warm smile gracing her lips.

Their eyes locked for a moment. To Branson Howard, time seemed to stand still as the captivating woman's ink-blue eyes sent a thrill leaping through him.

Ernie looked on, the mist that hung over his brain clouding his understanding.

The Ranger touched his hat and said, "I'm Branson Howard, ma'am."

Lucy caught her breath and responded, "My name is Lucy Daniels."

"Is it Miss or Mrs. Daniels?" he asked quickly.

"It is Miss." She blushed, placing the hat back on her head.

"Are you a resident of El Paso?"

"Not . . . not really. I live on a ranch on the other side of the mountains. But actually, I spent my childhood in Laredo."

The mention of Laredo made Branson's blood run cold. He had just met the most beautiful woman he had ever seen. Would his name strike a responsive chord in her memory? His reputation as Laredo's homegrown gunfighter might just turn her cold, if she knew about it.

Branson saw no recognition in her eyes, but he steered the conversation toward the horse races. Drinking in her beauty, he kept her talking. Meanwhile, Ernie returned to his task of carrying out the remaining flour sacks, while scowling at the man who was dominating Lucy's attention.

Down the street, the Taubert brothers rode up to the hitch rail in front of the Bank of El Paso and dismounted.

"You go ahead and cash the draft," Tommy said. "I'm going over to Hanson's. Meet you back here."

"Okay." Jack smiled and ducked under the rail, heading toward the bank.

The younger brother crossed the street toward Hanson's General Store. Dodging horses and vehicles, Tommy walked past Branson Howard and Lucy Daniels. At the door, he paused, allowing Ernie Carpenter to come through with a sack of flour in his hands. Shaking his head at the size of the man, he entered the store.

Inside the bank, Jack Taubert became the tail end of the line that had formed in front of the only teller's window. Directly in front of him stood Deputy Marshal Daryl Dunn, who was beside a well-dressed, middle-aged man.

Dunn looked over his shoulder and recognized Jack. "Oh, hello, Mr. Taubert," he said amiably. "We buried your friend Bud Hatch this morning. No services or anything."

"I understand," said Jack, his eyes finding those of the middle-aged man, who was observing his long hair with open distaste.

"Oh," said the deputy, "Mr. Taubert, this is Mr. Ebert. He is chairman of the El Paso town council."

Ebert nodded coldly at Jack. He did not offer his hand.

The line moved quickly, and soon Ebert stepped to

the barred window of the teller's cage. Jack moved up close to them, aware that others were now in line behind him. Unbuttoning his shirt pocket, he pulled out the draft.

The teller, a small, balding man of sixty, said, "Good morning, Mr. Ebert. I have the full amount all packaged for you."

Jack Taubert's alert eyes soon picked up that Ebert was withdrawing four thousand dollars in cash to be used as prize money in today's horse races. The deputy was accompanying him as bodyguard.

The teller slid a neatly tied package wrapped in brown paper toward the council chairman, who was signing a withdrawal slip. The wheels of avarice went into motion inside Jack Taubert's head. A little fast work with his gun could net him the whole bundle: *Four thousand dollars!*

Dunn and Ebert turned to leave. "See you around, Mr. Taubert," said the deputy.

Jack knew it was now or never. Stepping to the window, he cupped the draft in his hand, concealing it, and said to the teller, "I was going to cash a draft, but I seem to have forgotten it. I'll come back later."

Leaving the window to the next customer, Jack slipped the draft back into his pocket, buttoned it, and headed toward the door. Dunn and Ebert had just moved outside and were standing in momentary conversation on the boardwalk.

Whipping out his revolver, Jack headed through the door.

Chapter Nine

Lucy Daniels's attention was drawn away from Branson Howard by Ernie Carpenter, who dropped the last sack in the wagon, and said, "We are ready to go, Miss Lucy."

"All right." She nodded, giving Ernie a quick smile. Looking back at the strikingly handsome man, she said, "It has been nice meeting you, Mr. Howard."

"May I help you into the wagon?" asked the Ranger, offering his hand.

Ernie had started toward Lucy to assist her, but stopped when he saw the stranger doing so. His dull eyes sharpened, exhibiting his annoyance.

Tommy Taubert emerged from the general store into the brilliant sunlight, brushed past Ernie Carpenter, and crossed the street. He noted Jack's empty saddle, but swung into his own. He was watching the huge man in the bib overalls untying the wagon team when he heard the bank door squeal on its hinges. The sound pulled his gaze around, and he saw Deputy Dunn and the council chairman step through the dark opening.

They stood talking for a moment. The door came open again, and Tommy blinked at what he saw, going numb in disbelief. Jack stepped up behind the deputy, gun in hand, and brought the barrel down savagely on his head. Dunn's big hat absorbed some of the blow, but he went down, dazed.

Lining the muzzle between Ebert's eyes, the yellow-haired outlaw barked, "Gimme that package!"

The frightened council chairman complied immediately. Daryl Dunn was rolling on the plank sidewalk, shaking his head. At the same instant, Jack Taubert heard somebody on the street yell, "Robbery!" as he headed for his horse, clutching the money.

Tommy was dumbfounded. He felt like he was in the midst of a nightmare.

Jack was about to climb aboard his mount, when he saw the council chairman pull a small revolver from inside his coat. Raising his gun, Jack fired. Ebert buckled, his own gun sending a bullet into the dirt. The shots reverberated noisily among the clapboard buildings.

Across the street Lucy Daniels was standing in the wagon, about to sit down. The sudden loud reports frightened the wagon team, and the horses lunged into harness, bolting. The wagon's sudden lurch toppled Lucy from her standing position. She flew into the air and came down hard on the street, banging her head.

As the wagon careened away down the street with Ernie pulling on the reins, Branson Howard dropped to his knees beside the unconscious Lucy. Horses and wagons in motion on the street blocked his view of the shoot-out.

Just then, Daryl Dunn rolled over on the boardwalk, bringing his gun to bear. Jack Taubert's horse had pulled loose from the rail in fear. The outlaw was attempting to get hold of the reins and climb aboard, fumbling because of the money in one hand and the gun in the other.

Deputy Dunn was still groggy. He shot at Jack and missed.

Jack steadied himself, took aim, and fired. The bullet centered Dunn's forehead, spraying blood as it exited the back of his skull.

Next door to the bank was the Rio Grande Hardware Store. Adjoining the hardware store on the far side was Jim Bandy's Barbershop.

Jack Taubert's frightened horse was whinnying and dancing about, eyes bulging. With gun smoking, Jack was having a difficult time getting aboard. His voice cut the air. "Tommy! Let's get out of here!"

The sound of his name brought young Taubert from his stupefied bewilderment. His head whipped around.

At the same moment, Ralph Sloan, the proprietor of the hardware store, bolted through his door, brandishing a long-barreled revolver. In his excitement, he stumbled, and the gun discharged. The bullet plowed dirt across the street only inches from Lucy's head.

Ranger Branson Howard was about to leap up and get into the thick of the fight, but the stray bullet changed his mind. He knew he must take Lucy somewhere out of danger. People were scattering for cover as Branson hoisted the limp form of Lucy Daniels into his arms and carried her quickly toward Hanson's store.

Jack Taubert finally settled into his saddle. Sloan snapped back the hammer of his long-barreled revolver again. He was taking aim at Jack when Jim Bandy came out of his barber shop, raising the black muzzle of a shotgun. The face of an aproned customer appeared behind the shop's large plate-glass window.

Tommy was suddenly and unintentionally caught up in the violence. Jack's gun roared at Ralph Sloan as Jim Bandy, the barber, took aim at Jack's back with the shotgun.

Instinctively, to protect his brother, Tommy Taubert's hand grabbed for the iron at his hip. Whipping it out, he pointed it at the barber and fired. The impact of the bullet tearing through his body drove Bandy backward into his plate-glass window. The shotgun boomed, sending its charge into the boardwalk, as the barber crashed through the window, shattering glass in every direction.

Tommy heard Jack yell something at him. With his head spinning and his gun smoking, he stared at the motionless form of Jim Bandy draped over the foot-high windowsill. He turned to look for his brother and saw him galloping westward out of town. Spurring his horse, he quickly left the stunned crowd behind.

As the Taubert brothers thundered past the Lone Star Stagecoach office, Henry Yates and Bill Storey stood just outside the door. They had observed the entire scene.

Ranger Branson Howard had now emerged from the store with Lucy in his arms and was hurrying down the street past the crowd that was gathering around the fallen men. He knew she could be seriously injured from the way she had struck the ground and must have immediate attention.

Halfway to the office, Branson saw Dr. Aaron Finch coming toward him, black bag in hand. One of El Paso's citizens, who had gone to get the physician, was by his side.

As they drew abreast, Branson said, "Doctor, she could be in bad shape!"

"Is she shot?" asked Finch.

"No. Unconscious. She took a blow on the head. Fell from a wagon. Horses bolted when the shooting started."

"Take her on to the office," the elderly physician said, looking at Lucy's pallid face. "Put her on the examining table and bathe her face with water. When she comes around, don't let her move. I'll be back as soon as I can."

The deeply concerned Texas Ranger hurried to the office and laid Lucy on the waist-high table. Setting a basin of water on a small cart nearby, he soaked a cloth and pressed it gently to her face and brow.

"Come on, beautiful lady," he whispered. "Please wake up."

Within a few minutes, Lucy began to stir. A moan escaped her lips. "Miss Daniels," Branson urged. "Can you hear me?"

The lovely brunette's eyes fluttered for a moment and then focused on the tanned features of Branson Howard.

"Remember me?" he asked.

"Yes, of course," she responded, a shaky hand going to her forehead. "What happened?"

"You were thrown from the wagon when a gunfight broke out in front of the bank. Horses bolted, and you landed on your head."

"Where am I?"

"Doctor's office. He's tending to the men who got shot. He'll be here as soon as he can."

Lifting her head, Lucy said, "Would you help me sit up?"

"It's best that you don't," Branson said gently. "The doctor told me not to let you move when you regained consciousness. You hit the ground pretty hard, little lady."

Lucy nodded, relaxing, and looking deep into his eyes. Both of them felt the same sensation as before.

A bit frightened by it, Lucy broke the spell by saying, "Could . . . I have some water?"

Branson was giving Lucy small sips of water from a tin cup when Bill Storey entered the office, followed by Ernie Carpenter. The big man did not like this stranger, but he understood that the man was helping Lucy.

Lucy spoke to both of them, introducing Branson.

"Are you all right, Miss Lucy?" asked Ernie.

"I'll be fine," she answered with a faint smile.

"I'm sorry you fell," he said slowly, looking as if he would break into tears. "It's my fault. I didn't hold the horses still."

"It is not your fault, Ernie," she assured him. "No one could have held the horses when they were frightened like that."

Footsteps were heard at the door. Several townsmen appeared, carrying the council chairman and the barber. Dr. Finch came in behind them and crossed to where Lucy lay, while Ebert and Bandy were being carefully laid on cots. The two men were alive, but in serious condition.

Looking down at the lovely young woman, Finch said, "I'm glad to see you awake, miss. Are you in pain?"

"Just a headache, is all," she replied.

The doctor explained that Ebert and Bandy were critical and that he must remove the slugs from their bodies immediately. Lucy must be examined, but it would have to wait until he finished with the two wounded men.

All but two of the townsmen left the office. The ones remaining quietly carried on a conversation with Bill Storey and Branson Howard while the doctor worked on Ebert and Bandy. They explained that Marshal Bart Langford had just returned to town and would soon be gathering a posse to go after the two killers. Ralph Sloan and Deputy Daryl Dunn were both dead, and witnesses said the killers looked like brothers.

An hour later, the elderly physician wiped his sweaty brow and went to the basin to wash blood from his hands. "It's doubtful either one of them will make it," he told the group. "The next twenty-four hours will tell the story."

Commanding the two townsmen to keep a close eye on Ebert and Bandy, Finch turned his attention to Lucy. The weary doctor examined her carefully and said she was all right. She had a mild concussion, but could go home.

As they prepared to leave, Ernie stepped close to the young woman and said, "I will carry you to the wagon, Miss Lucy."

Storey and Branson followed as the huge man cradled Lucy in his arms and started toward the door. As they were passing through it, they heard one of the townsmen say, "Doc, Jim just died."

Ernie carefully placed Lucy in the wagon seat, and Bill Storey mounted his horse. While Ernie was climbing aboard the wagon, Branson said to Lucy, "I'm in and out of this area periodically. Would it be all right, ma'am, if I called on you sometime?"

Lucy's dark eyes flicked to Bill Storey, then back to Branson. The Ranger detected the shadow of fear that showed in her eyes.

"You have been very kind to me," she said with a sincere smile. "I thank you from the depths of my heart. But—" their gaze locked briefly again, sending the same shudder through their hearts. "But . . . it would be best if you did not call on me."

Branson was sure that her eyes were saying something far different. As he touched his hat and stepped away from the wagon, he knew he must see her again.

Ernie shook the reins and clucked to the horses. The Texas Ranger stood in the middle of the street and watched the wagon pull away. He held his gaze on it until it passed from sight.

Marshal Bart Langford was gathering a posse in front of his office as Branson passed by on his way to see Henry Yates. The posse was in a dark frame of mind; the two killers would be hunted down like mad dogs.

Sitting down with Henry Yates in the Lone Star office, Branson told the agent that he wanted the stage to pull out for Austin the next morning. They talked about the killing and robbery for a few minutes and then the Ranger excused himself and went out the back door to the big barn. There, driver Sam Neff and shotgunner Ray Ringdon were working on the stage-coach behind closed doors.

Satisfied with the progress in the barn, Branson went to the bank. In the back room by the big safe, he discussed the upcoming journey with the three Pinkerton men.

With everything set for the journey, the muscular Ranger emerged from the bank and crossed the street. Entering the general store, he approached a rather stout, middle-aged woman who was behind a long counter filling a large jar with dill pickles.

The woman smiled. "May I help you, sir?"

"Yes, ma'am," he said, touching his hat brim. "Is Mr. Hanson in?"

"Not at the moment," she replied. "Won't be for a while, either. He's in the posse that's going after— Oh! I know you! You're the gentleman who carried Lucy Daniels in here when she was knocked out. Poor dear. Is she still with Doc Finch?"

"No, ma'am," Branson said, shaking his head. "The doctor examined her and said she is all right. They've taken her home."

"Well, I'm glad for that."

"Yes, ma'am." The Ranger smiled. "Would you happen to know where Miss Daniels lives?"

"She lives on the Turk Killam ranch," replied Mrs. Hanson. "Mr. Killam is her stepfather. Her mother is an invalid. Killam's place is due west after you ride around the southern tip of the Franklins, so that makes the ranch about thirteen miles from here. Can't miss it. Has Killam's name plastered in big letters on the gate. Place with a lot of cottonwoods around the house."

"Much obliged, ma'am," said Branson, backing toward the door.

Hastening down the street, Branson hurried to the livery. His heart was dictating to him. He must see Lucy Daniels before leaving for Austin in the morning. Whatever fear she had of him calling on her must be erased, and now was the time to do it.

The love-struck Ranger led Herb Nolan's blue roan onto the street in front of the livery and swung into the saddle. He muttered an oath at the blazing early afternoon sun as he rode west out of town

Lucy Daniels, Ernie Carpenter, and Bill Storey arrived at the Killam ranch just after one o'clock, sweaty and covered with dust.

Ernie was told by Storey to unload the wagon and unhitch the horses and then to clean the barn. Meanwhile, Lucy hastened inside and attended to her mother, telling her of the robbery and shoot-out in town. She left out the part about her fall, and though her thoughts had scarcely strayed from him, she did not mention Branson Howard. It had struck Lucy during the ride to the ranch that she never learned what the handsome man did for a living.

Turk Killam met Storey in front of the house, irked because Ernie and Lucy were so late in returning from town. He cooled down when Storey explained about the shoot-out and Lucy's fall. Then he grew angry again when he learned that it was Jack Taubert and his brother who pulled the robbery. Men in Killam's gang did not pull jobs on their own.

Storey explained that Deputy Dunn was one of the men left dead from the shoot-out. Marshal Langford was gathering a posse of El Paso's toughest men to track down the Taubert brothers.

Killam swung his fist and swore. He had been a fool for trusting Bud Hatch's friend. Now Jack Taubert knew about the gold shipment and the robbery plans.

Storey calmed his fears by pointing out that the Taubert brothers would not dare stay in these parts. Bart Langford had loved Daryl Dunn like a son, and he would track the deputy's killers with a seething vengeance. Even if the Tauberts fled into Mexico, the border would mean nothing to Langford. He would track them until he caught them.

"Look, boss," Storey said grinning, "the Tauberts actually did us a favor. They'll draw Langford out of town for us. Now we can stick to our original plan. It will probably take Langford a full day, maybe even longer, to run those guys down."

Turk Killam was smiling from ear to ear. "Yeah!" he said. "We need to get in there *tonight*! Round up the boys. I'll meet you in the house. We'll have a drink and make our plans."

Fifteen minutes later, the outlaws were sitting around Turk Killam's table, drinking whiskey. Ernie remained out at the barn. Dorothy was napping, having learned to sleep through loud conversations. Lucy was in the kitchen, putting away the groceries.

"We'll ride into El Paso and arrive there after dark," Killam told the gang. "When the town is bedding down for the night, we'll figure a way to draw one of these Pinkerton men to the front door of the bank."

"That ain't gonna be easy, Turk," spoke up Dirk Holstead. "Those Pinkerton agents are professionals."

"I'll think of a way," Killam said in a petulant tone. "Don't worry about it."

"Right," came Holstead's answer.

Addressing the whole group again, Killam said, "Once the safe is opened, we'll kill the Pinkerton guards. We ain't leaving any witnesses."

Suddenly Lucy was heard from the kitchen door. "Turk, why are you so cold-blooded? Isn't what you are doing bad enough? Killing three innocent men on top of it is cruel and senseless. Why don't you wear hooded masks? Then you wouldn't have to kill anyone."

A fierce glow struck Killam's dark, wicked eyes. His mouth pulled into a tight, truculent line as he growled, "Lucy, you butt out! Do you hear me? Go back in the kitchen and mind your own business!"

The gang members sat in silence, having no desire to interfere.

"Turk Killam, you are nothing but a vicious beast!" Lucy snapped back.

Killam's chair scraped the floor as he jumped up and stomped to where she stood. Lucy's eyes held him hard, and she showed no fear.

The sudden outburst brought Dorothy awake. She twisted her head to see her husband and daughter.

"You're an ingrate!" Killam roared at Lucy. "If it weren't for me, you wouldn't have food in your belly and a roof over your head! You ought to be grateful. But are you? No!"

"Oh, I'm grateful!" Lucy breathed hotly, her eyes flashing. "Grateful that you are not my real father! Believe me, mister, if there was a way to get my mother off this stinking place without hurting her, I would have taken her a long time ago!"

Killam's big hand lashed out and slapped her savagely. The force of the blow knocked her through the door and sent her sprawling across the kitchen.

Dorothy screamed. Out in the barn, Ernie's head came up at the shrill sound of Dorothy's cry. Dropping the scoop shovel in his hands, he plodded toward the house.

Swearing in anger, the bearded outlaw leader crossed the kitchen floor, snatching Lucy to her feet. Sinking his fingers into the front of her dress, he slapped her savagely.

Lucy fought back, her teeth showing like fangs. Both hands formed into claws and raked violently down his face, drawing blood. The stinging, raw furrows added fuel to his anger. He shook her hard, tearing her dress. She clawed him again.

Dorothy screamed for them to stop, while the other men sat numb and immobile.

Killam threw Lucy through the door into the large front room. Lucy rolled and slammed into an end table. A kerosene lamp sitting on the table tumbled forward and crashed.

Dorothy wailed, her voice filling the room. Lucy was scrambling to her feet, pulling the torn dress over her white shoulders as Turk headed toward her, blind with rage.

Suddenly the front door frame was filled with six-feet-seven inches and three hundred pounds of fury. The massive shadow caught Killam's attention immediately. He stopped cold, eyes bulging, jaw slack.

Ernie Carpenter resembled a vast, towering, formidable mountain. He watched Lucy move toward her mother's bed, clutching at her tattered dress, her hair tangled and disheveled. Killam was frozen on the spot.

The big man's gaze left Lucy and shifted slowly to the bearded outlaw leader. His normally dull eyes were alive with malignant heat. The rush of color to his face seemed ready to split the skin. Breathing hard, he said, "You hurt Miss Lucy. Now I am going to hurt you."

Throwing palms up, Killam stammered, "N-now, l-look here, Ernie. Lucy . . . Lucy is m-my daughter. I h-have to make her do wh-what I say."

The giant moved toward his prey. Bill Storey left his chair and stepped in front of him. "Settle down, Ernie," he gasped. "Miss Lucy will be all right. Don't—"

Ernie's massive arm swung and sent Storey crashing across the room. Then the furious man seized Turk Killam, picked him up, and hurled him out the wide front door.

Killam's two hundred pounds sailed across the porch, rolled over the edge, and struck the ground violently. Ernie was through the door, going after him, before the other men could react. Coming to their senses, they jumped up from the table.

Killam groaned with pain as the huge man swooped down on him like some giant prehistoric bird. Bill Storey stumbled to the door on the heels of the other three men, his head spinning.

Ernie now had Killam hoisted arm's length over his head, ready to slam him to the ground.

Hugh Pyle whipped out his gun, dogged back the hammer, and shouted, "Don't do it, lamebrain!"

Storey crowded up beside Pyle, saying, "Put that away, Hugh! I'll handle this."

Pyle took a step back as Storey squared himself in front of his big cousin, who eyed him warily. Killam was breathing shakily, suspended nine feet in the air.

"Ernie," Storey said, "do you remember what I told you? Mr. Killam makes it so we can have money and a place to live and food to eat. You mustn't do this."

Lucy appeared at the door, holding her hand to a throbbing, bruised cheek.

"He hurt Miss Lucy," said Ernie, strangling out the words. "I am going to hurt him. I'm going to hurt him *bad*."

"Make him put me down," Killam cried out. "Please."

"Ernie," Storey pleaded, "I'm your cousin. For *me*. Don't do it."

The big man studied his cousin for a long moment and then said, "Before I put him down, he has to promise never to touch Miss Lucy again."

"I promise!" shouted Killam. "I promise!"

Ernie revolved, spying Lucy in the doorway. "Miss Lucy . . ."

"Yes," she responded.

"Do you believe him?"

There was no answer.

"Lucy!" shouted the suspended man. "Tell him you believe me!"

"*Can* I believe you, Turk?"

"Yes! Yes! I'll never lay a hand on you again! I promise!"

After a long pause, Lucy said, "All right, Ernie. You can put him down easy. I believe him."

The tension eased as Killam was lowered gently to the ground. He was embarrassed. To cover it, he immediately began talking about the gold robbery. Knowing Lucy was listening, he announced that the gang would wear masks when they pulled the job.

Lucy left the men and returned to the house. Ernie followed her, wanting to make sure she was all right. She assured him that there were no serious bruises.

Looking down at her with tender eyes, Ernie said, "Mr. Turk promised he won't hurt you no more, Miss Lucy."

Lucy was dubious about it, but she would not tell Ernie. "Yes, he did," she smiled in spite of the bruises on her face. "Thanks to you."

"I have to go back to the barn, now," he said, turning toward the door. Then he stopped, turned back, and reached out a big clumsy hand and gently stroked her face. Tears glistened in his eyes. "I like you, Miss Lucy," came the unhurried words.

Blinking against the sudden moisture in her own eyes, Lucy Daniels reached up and squeezed the meaty hand. "I like you, too, Ernie," she said in a whisper.

As the massive form shuffled out the door, Lucy turned to her mother and said, "I'm going to take care of these bruises and put on another dress."

Dorothy was weeping. "Oh, Lucy," she begged, "please leave before he kills you. Certainly there is someone with whom you can be safe and happy."

The brunette thought briefly of Branson Howard. Then she said, "No, Mother. I will never leave you."

Chapter Ten

Tommy Taubert followed his brother out of El Paso at a full gallop, fighting a rush of nausea. How did this awful thing happen? Was it only a nightmare? Would he wake up in a moment and find that none of it was real?

Jack looked back and saw his brother swaying in the saddle. "C'mon, kid!" he shouted. "Get ahold of yourself!"

Heading west along the southern tip of the Franklins, the Taubert brothers drew close to the river. "I have to stop!" Tommy cried, already pulling rein.

Jack skidded his mount to a halt and wheeled around. Tommy was out of the saddle, doubled over and retching up what was left of his last meal.

"Hey, kid!" Jack exclaimed. "You did all right! You saved my life!"

Tommy straightened up, gave his brother a glassy stare, and gagged, doubling over again.

When Tommy was finished, Jack looked at his pallid face and said, "We'll cross the river here, kid. There'll be a posse on our tails pretty soon. I want them to think we went into Mexico. We'll ride south for a little while, then we'll double back, cross the river upstream, and head north. I know about a cave in the Franklins where we can hole up for a while."

Tommy regarded him with angry eyes. "You and your lies about going straight!" he blurted. "You had me believing you! Now look what you've done! Here I am running from the law for something I had no part in. Why, Jack? Why did you have to rob that man?"

"Look, I'm sorry," Jack said, twisting his face. "I didn't plan it. I just looked down, and there was all that money in his hand."

"And you just *had* to take it from him, didn't you?" rasped Tommy. "You couldn't leave it alone, because you're so stinking greedy!"

"We don't have time to stand here and jaw," Jack said, wheeling his horse toward the river. "That posse's coming. Let's go."

Marshal Bart Langford dismounted at the river's edge and studied the hoofprints leading into the water. The rest of the twelve-man posse remained mounted.

"I was right, boys," said the lawman. "They're heading into Mexico."

"Marshal, I think it's a trick to throw us off," spoke up Payton Roads, a retired lawman. "One of Ben Sanders's cowhands is a friend of mine. He's told me how that Taubert boy is stuck on Ben's daughter. Thirty years as a sheriff taught me a lot of things. One of them is that when an outlaw has a particular woman under his skin, he won't stray too far from her."

Langford rubbed his bushy mustache. "You're dead sure one of them was Tommy Taubert?"

"Absolutely," affirmed Roads.

"It was Tommy, all right," put in Clarence Palmer, El Paso's bootmaker. "I made him a pair of boots last year. Funny thing, though. He sure never seemed the outlaw type to me. Real friendly, polite, clean-cut kid."

"It *was* Tommy Taubert, Bart," said Oscar Nelson, the town's blacksmith. "I've seen him with Ben on several occasions. It just don't fit. Tommy's been building him a herd. Planning on having his own ranch someday."

"The other one has to be his brother," Roads said. "He looked a lot like Tommy, only older. Maybe the brother talked Tommy into turning outlaw."

"It happens," Langford nodded. "So you think Tommy might just show up at the B-Bar-S?"

"Experience tells me he will. I don't think they're going into Mexico at all."

"Okay," said Langford. "Let's give it a shot. We'll ride to the B-Bar-S first."

Going by Turk Killam's brief description of the hidden cave's location, Jack Taubert found it after a short search. The hole in the mountain's base was eight feet wide. The cave grew wider inside and was some fifty feet deep.

After the horses were unsaddled and tied to some creosote bushes just outside the cave, Tommy sat on the ground in the mouth of the cave, leaning against the stone wall. His face was grim. Jack stood nearby, counting the money he had taken from the council chairman. Completing the count, he smiled at his brooding brother and said, "Four thousand, kid! Tell me what your share ought to be, and it's yours!"

The younger Taubert lanced his brother with a look of raw fury. "I don't want any of your bloody money!" he nearly screamed. "I wish you were still in prison! None of this would have happened!"

"Aw, now, come on, kid," chuckled Jack hollowly, showing his yellow teeth. "I'm your brother."

"Don't remind me!" spat Tommy. "Some brother you are. You told me you were going straight. I never should have believed you. It's your fault that I killed a man today!" Ejecting a moan at the thought, he doubled over, feeling sick again.

Jack stepped close, laying a hand on Tommy's shoulder. "Look at it this way, kid. By shooting that barber, you kept your own brother alive. He'd have killed me with that scattergun, for sure."

Tommy raised his head and slapped Jack's hand away. With fire in his eyes, he hissed, "Keep your bloody hands off me!"

Jack's hair-trigger temper flared. "Don't get nasty with me, mister high and mighty!" he blustered. "I'm trying to make you feel better, and you don't appreciate it. Now, you just sweeten up, or I might decide to knock the insolence clean out of you!"

"I whipped you once today," Tommy muttered through his teeth.

"You just got lucky, little brother. Don't press your luck. You couldn't do it again."

"Get off my back or I will!"

Jack's foot shot out, driving a fierce kick into Tommy's ribs. Breath gushed from his mouth. He started to pull his feet under him, and Jack kicked him again. Tommy rolled across the mouth of the cave. In his rage, Jack came after him, aiming a boot at his face.

The younger brother dodged it, seizing the foot and twisting it violently. Jack went down with a howl.

Tommy rose to his feet, breathing hard. His ribs were on fire, and his face was flushed with heated passion. His lean, hard frame poised for battle.

Jack got up, favoring the twisted ankle. The rage within him stamped haggard lines on his narrow, craggy face. Cocking his fists, he growled, "I'm gonna teach you some respect."

In two long strides, the older man reached his brother, swinging a violent right. Tommy pulled his chin back, making the fist cut air. Jack swore, attempting to set himself again. He saw Tommy's punch coming and tried to block it, but he was too slow. Tommy's agile, well-honed body had become one hundred and sixty-five pounds of mean muscle and bone.

The rock-hard fist exploded against Jack's jaw with a force that sent him reeling away from the cave toward the spot where the horses were tied. With grim determination fueled by his flaming temper, Jack lifted himself to his feet. Tommy was on him in a flash. Bone met bone savagely, and the outlaw brother went down again, rolling against the base of a large boulder.

Doggedly, Jack clambered up the side of the boulder, bringing himself erect. There was a warm, salty taste in his mouth and a dancing haze across his eyes. Through the haze, he saw a dark figure closing in.

Swaying like a drunken man, he swung a fist at the figure.

Jack's shock-fogged senses had thrown off his timing and marred his depth perception. The fist found nothing but empty space. Abruptly, from somewhere out in the fog, a sledgehammer blow put out the daylight. The ground seemed to open up and swallow him.

When Jack Taubert awakened, he rolled over, swallowed blood, and focused his eyes on the tall, slender figure of his brother. Tommy was standing beside his horse, drawing up the cinch on the saddle.

The outlaw shook himself and rolled to his knees. His head was throbbing. "Hey, kid," he said past numb lips, "what are you doing?"

Tommy dropped the stirrup into place and turned a petulant stare on his brother. "I'm going back to town and give myself up. Maybe if I do that, the judge and jury will go easy on me."

Rising to his feet, Jack spit blood and said, "You're not thinking clear, little brother."

"I'm not like you, Jack," Tommy retorted. "I don't have a record. If I go back voluntarily, it will have to mean something in the eyes of the law. Besides, it wasn't me that put the gun on that man and took the money."

"You were with me," said Jack. "That's all they'll think about."

"Not if I go back."

"Hey, man! Like I said, you ain't thinking clear. We're not talking about robbery. We're talking *murder*. You killed that barber! You are a *murderer*, Tommy! A prison sentence is out of the question. They'll hang you!"

Tommy Taubert swallowed hard. His shoulders drooped. Jack was right. He would face a murder charge if he went back to El Paso. He was now a fugitive from the law.

A moan escaped Tommy's lips as he turned back to his horse. He moaned again, leaning his head against the saddle. Despair gripped him. His dreams of having his own ranch had gone up in smoke. *Gun smoke.*

Young Taubert's heart turned to ice. He would never see Melinda again. His whole life had crumbled around him like a sand castle struck by the swelling tide. And it was all because of Jack's wretched, evil greed.

Gripping the saddle, Tommy shook his head. The scene of the morning shoot-out was vivid in his mind. He could see Jim Bandy dashing through the barbershop door, raising the muzzle of the shotgun. His own brother would be Bandy's target. Tommy's gun was in his hand, belching fire, before he even realized it.

He relived the horrendous moment over and over: the rising muzzle of the twelve-gauge, the gun in his own hand, the feel of its buck against his palm, its sharp report, the boom of the shotgun, Bandy crashing through the big window, Jack's voice yelling something, the sound of Jack's horse galloping away.

Tommy shook his head again, still gripping the saddle. *What else could I have done?* he asked himself. *Jim Bandy was going to shoot Jack.* As much as Tommy despised Jack's ways, Jack was still his brother. Tommy could not just sit there and let Bandy kill him.

While Tommy fought to get a grip on himself, Jack rubbed his aching jaw and pondered the situation. He needed to get back to the Killam ranch. Killam would be wondering what had happened to him. Somehow, he had to get Tommy to remain here at the cave until the gang had stolen the gold. When they brought it to the cave, Tommy would be here to help him relieve the gang of the whole sixty thousand.

Jack picked up his hat, ran his fingers through his long, greasy hair, and dropped it on his head. "Hey, kid," he said softly.

Tommy turned around to face him, his eyes filled with despair.

"Look," said the older brother, stepping close, "I'm sorry for what I done this morning. If I could, I'd turn the clock back and change it. But you know I can't do that. I really am beholden to you for cutting down the barber to save my worthless life. You're mixed up in this thing now, like it or not. So we've got to stick together."

Tommy held his sky-blue eyes on Jack, showing no expression.

Putting a sincere tone in his voice, the older Taubert said, "Kid, all of this has done something to me on the inside. I really do want to go straight, but I need strength from outside of myself. You are the one who can give it to me. There's something good inside of you that's lacking in me. If you'll stick with me, I can make it."

Tommy, only half listening, did not respond.

"Tell you what," Jack said, pushing a lilt into his speech, "let's you and me ride to Tucson. That's far enough away from here, and there are plenty of ranches in that area. We'll hire on as punchers, and with you to help me, I'll become an honest citizen. Okay?"

Young Taubert smiled weakly, nodding without enthusiasm.

At his brother's weak smile and nod, Jack squeezed his shoulders and said, "Hey, that's the spirit!" Jack released his hold and continued, "Now, here's the situation, kid. I signed on with Turk Killam as I told you, and I've got the rest of my gear at his place. So I'll ride over there and get my stuff, and I'll use some of this money to buy us some fresh mounts and supplies from Killam. Meanwhile, you wait right here, where it's safe. I'll leave you some beef jerky and stuff from my saddlebags. I'm afraid you won't be able to go back to that ranch you're working at and get your own stuff—you're too well known and were probably recognized in El Paso. But I'll be back real quick—no more than a day or so—and we'll hightail it for Tucson. Okay?"

"Okay, okay," mumbled Tommy with a sigh, not really paying full attention.

"Great." Jack wheeled, walked to where his saddle lay on the ground, and pulled out provisions from the saddlebags. Handing them to his brother, he threw the saddle blanket over the horse's back and then set the saddle in place. Reaching under the animal's belly and running the leathers through the cinch ring, he said over his shoulder, "Tell you what, kid. We'll work our tails off at Tucson and get a little money ahead. Then we'll go to San Francisco."

Tightening the cinch, Jack turned around and added, "That's where the *real* money is, Tommy. San Francisco." The light of greed was in his eyes again. "Old brother Jack will make his fortune in San Francisco! I'll be rich, kid! Rich!"

Tommy began to snap out of his stupor and stood listening as his brother rambled on. He noticed how quickly "we" had turned into "I."

Laughing gleefully, the black sheep of the Taubert family said, "I'll have a big mansion overlooking the bay! I'll have a money room on the top floor, kid, so I can wallow in it while I watch the sun dance on the water! And when your old brother Jack cashes in his chips here on earth, you can have carved on my gold inlaid tombstone: Here Lies Jack Taubert. Died Rich."

A look of disgust etched itself on Tommy Taubert's young face. Jack was never going to change. Money was his religion and his life. He would do anything to get his hands on it, and he would go to any extreme to appease his ravenous greed.

Jack mounted up. "See you soon," he said as he rode toward the open country west of the mountains.

Tommy felt a wave of deep despair wash over him as Jack passed from view. He was numb in soul and body. His life was ruined. People in El Paso knew him, and word would soon get to the Sanders family to be on the lookout for him.

The sun was lowering in the sky. By now, no doubt, Melinda knew he was a fugitive, being hunted for murder. Dropping to his knees at the mouth of the cave, he braced his back against the cool rock wall and buried his face in his hands.

It was midafternoon. Ben and Evelyn Sanders sat on

the porch of their large ranch house, enjoying the stiff
breeze that whipped through the yard. They were discussing the long ride they had taken into El Paso with
their daughter and Lloyd Candler, only to be told upon
arriving that the races had been canceled due to the
theft of the prize money.

Ben was attempting to light his pipe against the
breeze when he heard the sound of galloping hooves
touch his ears.

"Looks like Marshal Langford," Evelyn said, squinting against the brilliant reflection on the sun-struck
land.

"Must be the posse," commented the rancher. "Killers must've come this way. Bart probably wants to see
if we've laid eyes on them."

Melinda came out of the house as the dozen riders
drew up in front of the house in a cloud of dust. She
stood beside her mother, wondering why the posse
would be at the B-Bar-S.

The rancher stood up to meet Langford as the lawman dismounted and approached the porch. "Howdy,
Bart," he said in a friendly manner.

"Afternoon, Ben," the marshal responded, looking
past him to the women. "Hello, Mrs. Sanders. Melinda." Swerving his gaze to the rancher, he said, "Ben,
you're a responsible resident of these parts. You'd always shoot straight with me, wouldn't you?"

Frowning quizzically, Sanders said, "Why would you
ask a question like that, Bart? You know me well
enough."

Langford lifted his hat and wiped his brow. "Under
normal circumstances I *wouldn't* ask. But in this case, I
have to."

"What are you driving at, Bart?"

Still holding his hat, the marshal eyed the rancher
levelly and said, "Has Tommy Taubert shown up here?"

Melinda and her mother exchanged glances.

"Not yet," answered Sanders. "Why?"

"There was a robbery in town this morning, Ben. It
included a gunfight in which my deputy was killed."

"I know about the incident," said the rancher. "But what's it got to do with Tommy?"

"He was one of the robbers," Langford replied flatly.

The shock of Langford's words threw Melinda back on her heels. "That isn't true, Marshal!" she blurted.

"I'm afraid it is, Melinda," said Langford, replacing his hat on his head. "Several people saw him, including some of the men in this posse. There were two of them. Witnesses said the other one looked enough like Tommy to be his brother. Real dirty, though. Hair clear to his shoulders. We're figuring he *was* Tommy's brother."

Sanders twisted around to look at his wife and daughter. Shock was in their eyes. Melinda felt like she had been kicked in the stomach by a mule.

Facing the marshal again, Sanders said, "You're right, Bart. He *is* Tommy's brother. Name's Jack. He was here with Tommy this morning."

Tilting his head, Langford asked, "But you haven't seen them since?"

"Nope."

"I'm leaving a couple of men here, Ben," said Langford. "Just in case they show up. I expect your full cooperation."

"Of course." Sanders nodded.

"We'll be back later. Let my men handle them if they show up."

The marshal named Clarence Palmer and Oscar Nelson to remain behind. Mounting up, he said, "Too bad about Tommy, Ben. I know you put a lot of stock in him. Just goes to show, people will fool you. He's the one that shot Bandy. He'll hang, for sure."

As the posse rode away, Ben Sanders felt sick about Tommy Taubert. There was consolation in his mind, however. He had the satisfaction of knowing that he had shown the good sense that very morning to tell Melinda to break off her relationship with him. Someday she would fully realize the wisdom of her father.

Nearby, Melinda was devastated. She could not believe what she had just heard. Hot tears burned her eyes and scalded her cheeks as the sound of thundering hooves faded away.

Chapter Eleven

"I don't care if you *did* meet her in town this morning," growled Turk Killam, "you can't see her now. Or any other time, for that matter. She has no time to see any men. She's busy cooking for my crew and taking care of her invalid mother."

Ranger Branson Howard ran his gaze over the cold faces that confronted him from the shade of the long, low-roofed porch. He recognized Bill Storey as the man who had been with Lucy and the big dull man in town.

"Seems to me she is old enough to make her own decisions about who she sees," said Branson stubbornly, sitting astride the blue roan.

Storey spoke up. "I heard her tell you in town not to come calling on her, Mr. Howard. I would say she *did* make up her mind about you."

"And I noticed that she didn't answer me until she glanced at you," Branson prodded. "I don't think it was the answer she really wanted to give."

Dorothy Killam could hear the conversation at the front porch from her bed. Calling to her daughter, who was in her bedroom at the back of the house, she said, "Lucy! Come here!"

Seconds later, Lucy appeared beside the bed. She had bruises on both sides of her face, but had replaced her torn dress with a fresh one. "What is it, Mother?"

"There is a man outside who came to see you. Says he met you in town this morning. Turk is giving him a bad time."

Lucy dashed to the door and set her eyes on the

handsome man on the back of the blue roan. Mixed emotions stirred within her. Branson Howard had hardly left her thoughts. She wanted desperately to see him again, but not *here*. The stronger emotion won out, and she stepped through the door, totally forgetting the black-and-blue marks on her face.

Branson's eyes shot past Turk Killam as Lucy came into view. The shadow of the porch hid her bruises, but not the smile that graced her lips.

Touching his hat, Branson returned the smile and said, "Hello, Miss Daniels."

Killam's head tugged around. He scowled at Lucy, who stepped past him into the sunlight, saying, "What brings you here, Mr. Howard?"

"I came to see *you*, ma'am," he replied directly. "I wanted to make sure you were all right after your fall in town." Furrowing his brow, he added, "What happened to your face?"

Raising a hand to a bruised cheekbone, Lucy flicked a nervous glance at Killam and said, "Oh, well, I was going down into the cellar after I got home and . . . and I guess I was still a little dizzy from my fall in town. I fell down the stairs. I . . . I guess this is my day for taking tumbles."

"Do you think you should see the doctor again, ma'am?" Branson asked with concern. "I'd be glad to go get him for you." He knew Lucy's face had been marked by something other than cellar stairs. And by the furtive glance she had given the ugly man with the beard, Branson was convinced that he had inflicted the bruises.

"All right," grunted Killam. "You've seen her. Now *vamoose*."

"There is no need to be rude, Turk," Lucy said bluntly. "Mr. Howard was quite nice to me in town today. I would like at least to give him a cup of coffee. Besides, I want Mother to meet him."

Killam hunched his bulky shoulders resignedly. He dare not raise his voice to Lucy. Ernie Carpenter was nearby at the barn, and sound carried easily in the hot desert air.

Setting her deep-blue eyes on Branson, Lucy said, "Please get down and come inside, Mr. Howard."

Killam and his men watched Lucy guide the muscular man through the door. When they were inside, the outlaw leader held his voice low and said, "I don't trust this dude. You know anything about him, Bill?"

"No," replied Storey. "Looks like a bank president, the way he's dressed. But he walks like a man who's always ready for trouble. He *was* mighty protective of Lucy, though. Picked her up and carried her to safety when she fell from the wagon and all that shooting was going on. Then carried her all the way to the doctor's office."

"I don't trust him," put in Hugh Pyle.

"Take a look in his saddlebags," Killam said quickly.

Pyle hastened to the roan and plowed his fingers into the saddlebags.

Lucy and Branson Howard were standing over Dorothy Killam's bed inside the house. Dorothy was repeating his name over and over, saying that it rang a bell. She had heard it in Laredo but could not remember in what connection. Branson was silently praying memory would fail her.

Suddenly, Hugh Pyle appeared at the door. In one hand was a revolver. In the other was a nickel-plated badge.

Branson's head snapped up at the sight of the muzzle leveled on his chest. Lucy gasped.

"Don't you move a muscle, mister!" hissed Pyle.

Killam now stood beside Pyle. The others quickly crowded through the door behind them.

Killam's eyes glinted. His thick lips were a scarlet line, pulled down in anger. "We've got us a sneaking Texas Ranger here."

A tingle coursed down Lucy Daniels's spine. She was surprised, but not unpleasantly so.

While Hugh Pyle held his gun steadily on the Ranger, Killam stepped up to Branson and pulled the gun from his holster. Eyeing him malevolently, he snarled, "So you were interested in Lucy, huh? Hogwash! You came here to spy on us! How'd you find out?"

Howard looked at him vacantly. "Find out what?"

"Don't try to snow me, Ranger!" snapped Killam. "You found out about us gonna steal that gold, didn't you?"

"What gold you talking about?"

Killam's dark countenance filled with fury. His hand lashed out and slapped the Ranger's mouth with a stinging blow. Branson's eyes blazed, but the ominous black muzzle in Hugh's hand held him in check.

"Don't play dumb with me!" growled Killam. "You're the Ranger that's planning to ride the stage to Austin, ain't you? Tell me, Mr. Howard, were you really gonna have the gold on that stage?"

"Who told you that?" demanded Branson.

Just then Ernie Carpenter entered the room. The dull-eyed giant, unaware of the situation, started to speak to his cousin, but Bill Storey silenced him immediately. Ernie slowly took in the scene. Fixing his baffled gaze on Branson Howard, he wrestled with the familiar features, trying to remember where he had seen the man before.

Responding to the Ranger's question, Turk Killam said, "I'm the one asking the questions. Now, how did you find out about us planning the heist?"

"Had to have been Henry Yates, boss," spoke up Dirk Holstead. "Who else could it be? Henry must've got cold feet. Decided to switch sides."

Turk Killam burst into a verbal rage, cursing Henry Yates and heatedly condemning his soul to hell.

"What if it wasn't Henry?" cut in Al Weems. "You've told the Ranger about him now."

Killam swore, saying it had to be Yates. "Besides," he added, "it don't make any difference. We're gonna kill this stinking Ranger anyway. We got no choice."

Terror shafted through Lucy Daniels's heart. "Turk, what are you saying?" she choked. "You can't murder this man!"

Stabbing a forefinger at Lucy's face, the bearded outlaw roared, "You keep out of this, girl!"

Big Ernie's huge body tensed. As he drew in his breath, the ominous sound filled the whole room. Killam's head whipped around. Eyes wide, he lowered his finger.

Turning slowly back to Lucy, Killam spoke in a low, steady tone. "There is no choice, here, girl. This Ranger is in the way. If I let him live, he could put me and my men in prison. What would happen to you and your mother?"

In anguish, Lucy cried, "Turk, please don't kill him!"

"Have to," he grunted. "Nobody's standing in the way of me getting that gold. *Nobody!*"

Grasping for straws, Lucy said, "Do you realize what you are dealing with? This isn't just some stray lawman. He's a Texas Ranger! They are relentless. They will trail him right to your door, Turk. You'll never get away with it!"

Because of Ernie's presence, Killam held his temper. Through clenched teeth, he said evenly, "Nobody's keeping me from t. .t gold."

"It will be mighty hard spending that gold when you're dangling at the end of a rope!" Lucy retorted.

A dead silence fell over the room.

Passing a hand across his face, Killam turned to his men. "Take the Ranger to the barn," he said resignedly. "Tie him up real good. We'll figure out what to do with him later."

Lucy looked on helplessly as Branson Howard was taken at gunpoint to the barn. Ernie remained with her, still trying to remember where he had seen the man in the fancy clothes. He followed Lucy into the kitchen, where she began preparing supper.

Turk Killam stood on the porch with Bill Storey and Al Weems. Killam bit the end off a cigar and lit it. As he was shaking flame from the match, Storey looked up at the rider coming toward the house and said, "Boss, you aren't going to believe this. Look!"

Killam almost dropped his cigar as he focused on the long yellow hair and sharp-featured face of Jack Taubert.

"Howdy, gentlemen." Jack grinned, reining in.

"I never thought I'd see you again," Killam said without a smile. "But since you're back, I have the privilege of firing you."

"Now, wait a minute, Turk," Jack said, dismounting, "I know I'm later getting back than I told you, but that ain't no reason to fire me."

Killam ejected a humorless chuckle. "I ain't firing you for being late. I'm firing you for doing side jobs when you're a member of my gang. And now I'm double mad because you are leading a posse to my front door by showing up here."

Jack pushed his hat to the back of his head and let his eyes stray toward the sunset. "Oh. I figured you might've heard. Ain't no posse on my tail, though, Turk. I sent them into Mexico. They'll be gone so long looking for me down there, they'll speak fluent Spanish when they get back. And, hey, I'm sorry about the side job. I didn't know that was forbidden. Won't happen again."

Turk Killam thought about the fact that he was already shorthanded and now would have to leave one man behind to keep an eye on the Ranger. He really did need Taubert. Though he didn't trust him fully, he would use him to help pull the gold heist and then have Hugh Pyle kill him before the loot was divided up.

"Okay." Killam clapped a hand on Jack's bony shoulder. "All is forgiven. If the posse does come by here, you'll have to take to the cellar."

Winking, Jack said, "Can I take your stepdaughter down there with me?"

"Sure," Killam laughed. "If you don't mind taking Ernie along!"

Pyle and Holstead returned from the barn, reporting that they had tied the Texas Ranger to one of the vertical beams that supported the hayloft. Pyle laughed, saying Branson either would have to break the rope or pull the barn down on top of him to get loose.

Jack Taubert showed interest in the Ranger, but Killam evaded the matter, asking him where his brother had gone. Jack replied that Tommy was hiding out at the cave Killam had told him about. There was nowhere else for him to go.

Killam made a mental note that he would probably have to kill *both* Taubert brothers now.

During the evening meal, Lucy felt Jack's eyes on her intermittently. Not once did she give him the satisfaction of looking at him.

The bearded leader sat directly across the table from Hugh Pyle. At one point he looked up at him and said, "Hugh, I'm gonna leave you here to keep an eye on the Ranger and to look after the women and the idiot."

Pyle stiffened in protest. "Aw, come on, Turk," he complained. "I don't want no nursemaid job."

Lucy's attention was drawn to the conversation.

"You'll get your cut of the gold the same as if you went with us," Killam assured him. "That Ranger could be dangerous. I figure the way you hate lawmen, he'll be in good hands." Knowing Lucy was listening, Killam said, "If that Ranger even looks like he's trying to escape, kill him."

Less than two hours later, Hugh Pyle stood on the porch and watched the gang ride away into the night. Branson's blue roan was still tied at a hitching post near the porch. Before pulling away, Killam's last words had been for Pyle to take the animal to the barn and turn it loose in the corral. Inside the house, Ernie Carpenter was washing dishes in his clumsy manner, while Lucy was feeding her mother.

Hugh Pyle's temper had been rubbed raw because of having to remain behind. When he released the reins from the post, the roan sensed the anger in his jerky movements. It whinnied, backing up quickly, and the leathers slipped from Pyle's hand. He swore loudly at the horse, seized the reins, and snapped them hard. This served only to frighten the animal more. Eyes bulging, the roan jerked its head up. Pyle swore again, repeatedly lashing the horse's face with the tips of the reins.

Lucy appeared at the door, with Ernie looking over

her shoulder. By the light coming from the windows, they could see what Pyle was doing.

Ernie stared at the scene incredulously. The outlaw was whipping the frightened animal's face without mercy, venting his anger. A muscle twitched in Ernie's jaw. Stepping around Lucy, the infuriated giant lumbered toward Pyle and the horse.

Lucy burst from the door and dashed past Ernie, screaming, "Hugh! Stop it! Stop it! Ernie's coming! He'll tear you apart!"

Pyle turned to face her in the gloom. Over her shoulder, he saw Ernie coming. His left hand still clung to the leathers. In his panic, he reached for his gun with the right hand, but forgot to let go of the reins. When the gun was coming from the holster, the roan jerked its head. The sudden snap of his body caused the gun to slip from his fingers. Letting loose of the reins, he dropped to the ground, feeling about for the weapon.

The outlaw felt powerful hands sink into his clothing, then he was sailing through the air. He hit the ground twenty feet from where he was launched. The angry, shuffle-footed giant was headed for him, growling like a grizzly.

Pyle got up to run, but his legs refused to cooperate. Ernie picked him up again, saying, "You are a bad man. You hurt the horse."

Pyle could hear Lucy calling to Ernie from somewhere in the dark as he pleaded, "No, Ernie! Don't hurt me! I'm s—"

The outlaw was airborne again. Three times he saw the lights of the house swirl around him before the black earth came up to jar him savagely.

Pyle's head was reeling when he heard the words "bad man" growled another time. He felt the strong hands again, lifting him. But this time, Ernie was walking and carrying him. Lucy's voice was close by.

"All right, Miss Lucy," came the thick-tongued reply.

Pyle felt himself drop and then abruptly he was engulfed in water. It was in his mouth before he could close it. Then it was in his nose, his lungs, and his ears.

Thrashing about in the large circular water tank, the outlaw found the edge and pulled himself out. He rolled on the ground, coughing and spitting water.

Suddenly, Lucy was beside him, helping him to his feet. "Hugh, you shouldn't have done that," she said. "Ernie goes wild when somebody hurts an animal."

"I'm gonna kill him!" gasped Pyle. "You hear me? I'm gonna kill him!"

"Hush!" she warned. "He's with the horse now. I've got them both quieted down. Listen to me. You'd better just forget this. Stop talking about killing Ernie. Even if you could do it, Bill Storey would kill you an inch at a time. And if he didn't, *I* would. Now go to the bunkhouse and put on some dry clothes. Come to the kitchen, and I'll give you some hot coffee."

Pyle limped to the bunkhouse while Lucy walked back to the house, where Ernie stood with the quivering animal in the spray of yellow light. He was hugging the roan's neck and gently stroking its long face, saying, "It's all right. The bad man won't hurt you no more. I promise. I won't let him hurt you no more."

When Pyle walked into the kitchen in dry clothes, Ernie was seated at the table with Lucy. Pyle's gun was lying on the table. Without comment, he slipped it into his holster and then eased into a chair as Lucy poured him a cup of coffee.

"Thanks." He smiled, noticing that Ernie had no coffee. Attempting to smooth things over, he said, "Don't you want some, Ernie?"

Ernie's ponderous head swiveled back and forth on his huge, bulky neck. "I don't like coffee."

Seeking to ease the tension further, Lucy chuckled and said, "I think Ernie is afraid it would stunt his growth."

With that, she rose and went to the oven. Pulling out a hot pan, she placed it on a tray, along with a table setting, bread, butter, and coffee cup. As Lucy placed the steaming coffeepot on the tray, Pyle asked, "You just now feeding your mother?"

"No," Lucy answered levelly. "She's asleep. It's for the Ranger."

"He can go hungry," Pyle said tartly.

"Look, mister," Lucy snapped back, "I'm not part of this vile gang of cutthroats. I still have my humanity. The Ranger is getting this food."

Pyle saw Ernie's listless eyes fixed on him. "Okay," he said, "but I'm going with you."

"There is no need for that," Lucy said politely. "I'm not going to let him loose. If I did, Killam would take it out on me, and there would be no one to take care of my mother."

"I don't believe you."

Fixing Pyle with a piercing stare, she said, "Put your thinking cap on, mister. Who was it that stopped Ernie from pounding you to a jelly a while ago? I could have let him kill you. Then I could have turned the Ranger loose, couldn't I?"

Pyle gave her a sullen look.

"I'm a prisoner, here, Mr. Pyle," Lucy said gratingly. "So is my mother. She can't be moved, so we're both stuck. I know my limits with Turk. If he found out I let the Ranger go, Mother would end up suffering. So you sit here with Ernie while I go feed him."

As Lucy carried the tray out the door with a lantern dangling from one finger, Dorothy Killam lay in her dark corner. She had heard the conversation. Hot tears washed her cheeks.

Branson Howard was working his hands in the darkness, trying to stir some circulation. His wrists were bound behind him around an eight-by-eight-inch beam. Ten feet above his head was the front edge of the hayloft.

Branson's head came up at the sound of the latch rattling at the barn door. He could see the yellow light of the lantern through the cracks. Presently, the graceful form of Lucy Daniels appeared. The door clicked shut, and she walked to him, leaving the lantern by the door. Setting the tray at his feet, she said, "Hello, Ranger. You hungry?"

"Yes, ma'am," he replied.

Returning with the lantern, Lucy hung it on a nail nearby. Stepping close, she said, "I wonder why they didn't tie your feet?"

"The way my hands are tied, it wasn't necessary. I suppose you are being watched."

"Yes," she said. "The gang has gone to El Paso to break into the bank and steal the gold while the marshal is chasing the killers. But my stepfather left one of his men behind. He'll be in to check on you later."

The lantern light reflected off Lucy's dark hair and illuminated her ink-blue eyes. They stared at each other as they had earlier in the day, the same indescribable sensation there again.

Lucy hesitated and then said quietly, "I'll have to feed you."

While she fed the trussed-up Ranger, Lucy explained her predicament at the ranch. She filled him in on Turk Killam's crimes and the caper that was being pulled at the moment.

Branson asked about the ruckus with the horse earlier, and she explained about Ernie Carpenter and the way he protected animals and herself. She added that the roan did not seem to be harmed too badly, just frightened a bit.

Finishing, Lucy said, "So you see, Mr. Howard, we've got to figure a way to set you free so it looks like you did it on your own. Any other way, and my mother ends up suffering severely if Turk gets back here without being arrested."

"I understand, ma'am," Branson said softly. "If the robbery is successful, they could be back sometime after midnight, right?"

"More like dawn," Lucy answered. "They're taking the gold to a cave somewhere in the Franklins. No doubt they'll celebrate for a while." Leaning down, she placed the empty coffee cup on the tray and then stood up. Her eyes sparkled. "I've got it!"

"Hmm?"

"Ernie! I will tell him that you are my very dear friend and that I will be terribly hurt if you are harmed by Turk. He will do anything to keep me from being hurt. While Pyle is out here checking on you, I'll convince Ernie to go out and put the roan in one of the stalls over there, to make it feel better."

"But what about Pyle?"

"I'm sure he will sit up all night waiting for the gang to return. He'll probably stay right there in the house and make me sit up with him."

"That's what I mean," said Branson. "Won't he get suspicious if Ernie goes outside? I would think he'd want him in sight also."

"Ernie would just go to sleep, and Hugh knows it. Ernie has his own shack where he sleeps, near the toolshed. He snores so loudly, nobody can stand it. Pyle will assume he is going to his shack. Ernie will be eager to make the roan more comfortable. When he comes, you ask him to untie you. If Turk should come back after you're gone, he'll question all of us, including Ernie."

"Won't Ernie tell Turk that you sent him out here?"

"To take care of the horse, yes. Certainly it wouldn't be my fault if you coerced him into untying you. Even if you had told Ernie that Turk was going to hurt you if he didn't untie you, it would be the truth, and there would be no connection with me."

"Okay." Branson nodded. "It's worth a try. If I could only guarantee that I could catch and arrest Turk before he returns here, all this would be unnecessary. You could untie me and let me go. But since there is no such guarantee, I'll be waiting for Ernie."

"It will work, Mr. Howard." Lucy smiled.

"Sure, ma'am." He smiled back.

For a moment there was silence between them, and their eyes locked again. On impulse, the beautiful woman moved close to him. The Ranger's heart leaped.

Breathing softly, she half whispered, "You don't have

to call me ma'am. You can call me Lucy." She paused as they stared at each other.

"I must go now," she said in a low tone. "Ernie will be here within an hour or so. I'm sorry you have to stay in that position until then."

"Don't worry. I'll be all right."

Carrying the lantern and the tray to the door, she unlatched it and then turned around to look at him. She looked captivating in the soft glow.

"You don't have to call me Mr. Howard," he said. "You can call me Branson."

She smiled and then closed the door and hurried away.

Chapter Twelve

While Hugh Pyle was out of the house checking on Branson Howard, Lucy talked to Ernie as planned. She went over the instructions several times, making him repeat it back until she was sure that he knew he must put the horse in the stall before going to his shack for the night. She particularly stressed that he must keep it a secret from the bad man who hurt the horse.

A few minutes later, Hugh Pyle strode into the kitchen, where Lucy and the big man sat at the table. He positioned himself opposite them, pulled out his gun, dogged back the hammer, and pointed it threateningly. Ernie scowled and started to get up.

"Sit down!" snarled Pyle.

Ernie kept rising.

"Better make him sit down, Lucy," said the outlaw. "I just made a decision. I'd rather face Bill Storey for killing his molasses-brained cousin than to face Turk Killam for letting that Ranger get loose. Somehow I got a feeling that you two might try to put something over on me."

Lucy's heart was in her throat. "What on earth could we do?" she asked. "You know I wouldn't do anything to endanger my mother."

"Old Hugh just ain't taking any chances, honey. Call it a hunch. But whatever you call it, you and the mobile mountain are sitting right here with me till Turk walks through that door. Now tell him to sit down."

* * *

A few people were still milling about on the streets as the Killam gang rode into El Paso. San Francisco Street was well lighted [1] kerosene lanterns that hung on the fronts of stores and shops. The riders pulled their hats low to shadow their faces. Moving slowly along the street so as not to attract attention, they spoke in low tones.

"I like your idea, Jack," said Turk Killam. "That ought to get us in the bank slick as a whistle. You've got brains."

"Some of us do, some of us don't," Jack responded dryly.

Killam noticed a man walking along the boardwalk in the same direction they were heading. "Evening, sir," he called.

"Evening."

"We've been on the trail. Ran into some folks that told us you had some excitement here this morning."

"Sure did. Robbery. Shoot-out. Three men dead."

"Catch the killers?"

"Don't reckon. Leastwise the marshal and his posse ain't back yet. I'd know if they was. My son's in the posse."

"Sure hope they catch them."

"Yeah. Me, too. Ain't had a hanging here in a couple of months."

As the five riders approached the bank, Jack noticed that the big window at the barbershop was boarded up. Turning at the corner, they rode up into the alley behind the bank. They dismounted quietly, pulling hooded masks from under their belts.

"Okay, Jack," Killam said in a low voice, "take Al with you, and the rest of us will meet you shortly at the front door."

Jack Taubert and Al Weems pulled the hoods over their heads and made their way quickly along the side of the stone building toward the street. The moon was up now and cast eerie shadows about them.

Pausing at the corner of the building, they peered up and down the street. The man Turk had talked to earlier was turning the corner, heading down a side street.

"Maybe we ought to use him," Weems said.

"Okay," agreed Jack, "let's— Hold it!"

The last saloon was closing up a few doors away. Several half-drunk cowboys were coming through the swinging doors, laughing and jesting. After one boisterous outburst of laughter, they climbed aboard their horses and rode away. At the same moment, the bartender appeared at the door, shoving a small elderly man ahead of him.

"You go on home, Benny," came the bartender's voice along the lantern-lit street.

The old man swayed on shaky legs. His eyes were bleary. "Let's see, Sam," he slurred, "which way is it?"

The bartender turned him in the direction of the spot where Jack Taubert and Al Weems stood. "That way, Benny. Good night."

"Perfect!" whispered Jack. "You grab him when he comes by. Be sure to cover his mouth. I'll get the lanterns."

No one was on the street when Weems seized the old man, clamping a hand over his mouth. He dragged him into the shadows while Jack rushed along the boardwalk and lifted two burning lanterns from their nails. Within seconds, he had returned to where Weems held his wide-eyed, frightened captive.

Jack doused the flame in one of the lanterns, removing the cap from its tank. At the same instant, Killam and the others appeared, wearing their hoods.

"Okay," Jack said, "let's go."

The gang gathered in front of the bank door. Jack removed the glass flue, exposing the flame.

Turk Killam banged his fist on the door. "Hey, you inside the bank!" he bellowed. "We've got a problem out here! Come to the door!"

Footsteps were heard inside. Instantly, Jack Taubert began pouring kerosene over the old man's head. Weems had removed his hand from the man's mouth, and

Benny ejected a pitiful wail, blinking against the stinging liquid that ran into his eyes.

Abruptly, the shade on the door window moved, and a face appeared. The Pinkerton guard's eyes bulged as he saw the hooded man dousing Benny with the flammable liquid.

Holding the burning second lantern in a threatening manner, Jack said to the Pinkerton man, "Open up, or I'll turn this old duffer into a human torch!"

The guard hesitated.

"I mean it!" snarled Jack, shoving the naked flame dangerously close to the old man's kerosene-soaked hair.

The lock rattled, and the door swung open. Turk Killam and his men rushed through the door, guns drawn. Jack stayed with Benny.

Moonlight through the windows sufficiently illuminated the interior of the bank for Killam to make out the other two guards standing at the door to the back room. They had a clear view of Jack Taubert and the whimpering old drunk, and they offered no resistance.

"Get their guns," Killam ordered, motioning to Storey and Holstead.

The weapons were quickly collected. Jack pushed the old man through the door and closed it. Forcing him to the back of the bank, he glanced at the huge vault door and said to the Pinkerton men, "Okay, open it. No sass, or you'll watch this guy burn."

Running his gaze over the hooded masks, the guard who had opened the door saw desperate eyes through the round holes. "We can't open the vault," he said nervously. "We don't have the combination."

Jack moved the flame toward Benny's head. "You got three seconds to start opening that safe, mister!"

"I'm telling the truth!" said the guard.

"Who's got it, then?" demanded Killam.

"The bank's president," came the hasty answer.

"You know where he lives?"

"Yes. He's only a few blocks away."

Nodding toward Bill Storey but careful not to speak his name, the outlaw leader said, "This man is going to

take you to the president's house. Get him here fast."
Swinging his hooded face back to the guard, he warned,
"No funny stuff. If you're not back here in twenty
minutes, this old man burns to a cinder, and so do your
pals." In a moment, Storey and the guard were gone.

Benny's whole body trembled. He had sobered con-
siderably. Looking into Jack Taubert's eyes through the
holes in the mask, he said, "I ain't done nothin' to you,
mister. You got no call to burn me if these guys don't
cooperate with you."

"Shut up," Jack said flatly. "Any more lip from you,
and I'll stick your fingers into the flame."

One of the two remaining guards lost control of his
temper. "You're real tough stuff, aren't you?" he challenged. "I suppose you're good at beating up women,
too. Helpless old men and defenseless women. Yep,
that's your style, isn't it? If you had to face a real man,
your guts would turn to sour milk."

"Shut your trap, mister!" Jack said, whipping the
words at the man. "Any more out of you, and *you'll* be
the first torch!"

"Sure," came the guard's retort, "as long as you've
got your buddies with you. If it was you and me alone—"
His words were cut off by the other guard touching his
arm and telling him to let it go.

Silence fell over the room. Jack Taubert set his greedy
gaze on the big vault door. Behind that mass of pol-
ished steel lay enough gold to make him a very rich
man. A warm satisfaction washed over him as he remembered Tommy waiting at the cave. The moment
Jack threw his gun on the gang, little brother would
jump right in to help him. What else could the kid do?
After all, Jack was his brother, and blood is thicker than
water. Tommy had proved that when he shot the barber this morning.

It took almost twenty minutes for Bill Storey and the
Pinkerton guard to return with bank president Frank
Rainey.

Fifteen minutes later, the gang rode away in the
moonlight, leaving Rainey, the guards, and the old man

bound and gagged. The two hundred pounds of nuggets were in eight canvas bags of twenty-five pounds each, which were divided among the saddlebags of the gang.

Silver moonlight sprayed the desert as, nearly two hours later, the five happy riders approached the heavy stand of mesquite that blocked the cave entrance. They had pulled it off without a hitch. The gold was theirs.

Jack Taubert tensed as they rounded the mesquite. He would go into action the moment he could maneuver himself away from the others and get next to Tommy. The two of them would head toward Tucson that very night.

As they rounded the mesquite in the light of the moon, Jack's eyes swung toward the cave. Tommy's horse was not at the creosote bush. Quickly his gaze swept the area, but the animal was nowhere in sight. He felt his body stiffen.

Turk Killam's deep voice broke the silence. "I thought you said your brother was here, Jack."

"He was when I left," he replied, straining his eyes at the dark mouth of the cave. "Tommy!" he called while dismounting. "Hey, Tommy! You in the cave? It's Jack!"

There was no response.

"Looks like he cut out on you, Jack," said Bill Storey.

"Forget him, Jack," said Killam, breaking into a laugh. "Hey, hey! We've got the gold, and I've got whiskey! Let's celebrate!"

Jack Taubert felt a surge of anger. Tommy had run out on him. The witless kid had probably decided against Jack's advice and had gone to turn himself in. *Man that's got a conscience is a fool*, he thought. *Well, let him go. He'll wish he had stuck with me when he's taking the plunge to the end of that rope.*

At the entrance to the cave, the outlaws formed a circle as Turk Killam produced a bottle from his saddlebags and popped the cork. "C'mon, boys," he said, laughing heartily. "Let's have a round. Then we'll open the bags and have a look."

Jack joined the circle, knowing he would have to take

the gold from the gang by himself. The men were jubilant. They laughed and joked while passing the bottle, each one pouring the whiskey down freely.

"I've brought along enough food and water for two men for three days," spoke up the bearded leader. "Weems and Holstead will stay here with the gold, while the rest of us go back to the ranch and make things look normal. I'll send out more provisions later. As soon as things cool down, we'll take the gold to the ranch and divide it up."

While the bottle continued to change hands, Killam went to his horse and pulled one of the heavy canvas bags from his saddlebag. "Gather around, boys," he said, laughing hoarsely, "let's take a gander at the loot."

Killam dropped to his knees and began to untie the bag.

"One thing, Turk," said Jack, watching Killam's thick, stubby fingers fumble with the strings.

"What's that?" he mumbled.

"If you leave Weems and Holstead here with the gold, what's to keep them from taking off with it?"

"*Fear,*" came the outlaw leader's ready answer. "They'd have a hard time enjoying it with ol' Turk Killam on their trail. They know I'd track them to the ends of the earth if I had to."

Jack saw his chance. All four men were clustered in one spot, their eyes transfixed on the canvas bag. Slowly, he inched himself backward.

Still working at the strings, Killam guffawed and added, "Hell, Jack, you'll soon learn that nobody crosses Turk Killam. No man's got them kind of guts!"

Suddenly there was a burst of gleeful laughter among the four as shiny golden nuggets spilled into the moonlight.

Jack Taubert was now positioned a dozen feet away. His cold voice cut through the excited voices. "*Killam!*"

From his knees, the bearded outlaw turned toward the voice. The smile on his thick lips drained away when he focused on the black muzzle that stared at him like a single menacing eye.

The dry double click of the hammer being eased back was magnified in the sudden deathly silence. Storey, Weems, and Holstead were frozen like statues.

Jack's face was slick and wicked in the pale light. "You're wrong, Killam," he said heavily. "One man's got them kind of guts."

A deep growl emerged from Killam's thick lips. "Why you—"

"Shut up!" barked Jack. "Drop the nuggets back in the bag and tie it up." Swinging cold, calculating eyes on the others, he said, "First dude that moves without me telling him to goes to hell on the spot. Storey, you reach down real slow-like and lift Turk's gun out of its holster."

Cautiously, Storey did as he was told.

"Now," said Jack, "toss it over there in the cave. Remember, the bullet is quicker than the hand."

Killam's eyes glinted with venom as Storey threw his revolver into the dark void of the yawning cave.

"Now do the same with your own," commanded Jack.

"Taubert!" roared Killam from his knees. "I'll hunt you down! I'll take you apart a piece at a time!"

"Not if you're dead, you won't."

Storey was carefully lifting his gun from its holster.

Abruptly, Killam shouted, "Don't give him your guns! He's gonna kill us all!"

Storey gripped his revolver in response, bringing it up for action. Jack's gun spit fire. Storey buckled as the slug struck his midsection, and he dropped to his knees. Al Weems's hand started down for his gun.

"Hold it!" snapped Jack, lining the smoking weapon on him. Weems froze.

Bill Storey gave it a final effort. His revolver was still hanging from his fingers as he clutched the wound with his free hand. Summoning strength like a dying beast, he brought the weapon up. Jack saw the movement, swung his gun on Storey, and fired again. The slug tore into Storey's heart. He teetered momentarily and then pitched forward, his face slamming the ground.

Both Weems and Holstead had started to draw, but checked themselves as the deadly muzzle quickly lined on them. "Throw your guns in the cave," Jack commanded, and this time they complied immediately.

Turk Killam's whole body burned with wrath. Standing up slowly, he hissed, "I'll get you, Taubert. If it's the last thing I ever do, I'll get you!"

"You get back down on your knees," Jack demanded, cocking his gun and lining it between Killam's eyes. "Now, I'm not a cold-blooded murderer, Turk, but I swear I'll drop you where you stand." When Killam did not immediately comply, a savage look leaped into Jack's face. Eyes bulging, he sprayed saliva, blaring, "On your knees, Turk! Now!"

The bulky man blinked, as if he expected the gun to fire. Sweat beaded his brow as he dropped to his knees.

Barking commands at Weems and Holstead, Taubert held his gun on Turk Killam. If the two men failed to do exactly as he directed, he would blow their boss's head off.

Within ten minutes, all the gold was loaded on Turk's horse and all their revolvers were packed in Jack's saddlebags, except one, which he stuck under his belt. The other three horses were put on a lead rope. Jack was now ready to leave. Holding them at gunpoint, he said, "Okay, boys, off with your boots and your socks!"

From his kneeling position, Turk Killam fixed his blazing eyes on the skinny man. "Taubert!" he boomed. "You're not gonna leave us here with no horses and then take our boots, too!"

"*And* your socks," Jack said coolly.

Moments later, Jack mounted his horse, holding the lead rope. Boots, stuffed with socks, including Bill Storey's, were tied to the saddles. As he eyed the three men standing in their bare feet, his laughter echoed off the surrounding rocks. "Good-bye, boys! Have a nice walk! I'm rich! Rich!"

Killam, Weems, and Holstead cursed at Jack Taubert

as he and the horses disappeared into the night. His hollow laughter taunted them. They could hear him repeating it over and over, until he finally passed from earshot: *"I'm rich! I'm rich! I'm rich!"*

Chapter Thirteen

Posse members Clarence Palmer and Oscar Nelson sat on the front porch of the huge ranch house with Ben Sanders, discussing the situation. The moon shone like a great silver disc in the night sky. The two possemen rolled cigarettes, while Sanders fired up his pipe.

"Too bad about your little gal taking this so hard, Ben," said Palmer, El Paso's bootmaker.

"She'll get over it, Clarence," replied the rancher. "Tommy has a magnetic personality, and Melinda just let herself get a little too attached to him. Wyman Candler's son, Lloyd, is quite interested in her. I'm sure he'll be able to heal any wounds she might have."

"Gonna hurt you to lose such a good worker, though, ain't it, Ben?" said Nelson, the blacksmith.

Sanders shook his head sadly. "You're not kidding, Oscar. I've never had one quite like Tommy. Workingest devil you've ever seen. I was planning on making him foreman when old Charlie Thomas retires." Pausing a moment, he said wistfully, "I just don't understand it. I would've trusted that boy with my last dollar."

"Is that brother of his known to be a bad one?" asked Palmer.

"To tell you the truth, I didn't even know Tommy *had* a brother," came the rancher's reply. "He never mentioned him. All of a sudden, he shows up right here on this porch this morning, long greasy hair and all. Wears his gun low and thonged down. Has a mean look in his eye."

Nelson abruptly sat up straight, squinting eastward.

"What is it?" Sanders asked, looking off in the same direction.

"Something moving out there," Nelson said, lowering his voice.

"Sure enough," agreed Palmer. "It's a rider."

The three men watched the horse and rider move slowly closer. After a full minute, Ben Sanders said, "It's Tommy!"

The two possemen whipped out their guns and crouched behind the porch railing. "Better get down, Ben," whispered Palmer. "This could get bloody!"

"Doesn't appear he's coming for a fight, fellas," said the rancher. "There's no gun in his hand. Just get down out of sight. I'll stand up when he reins in and speak to him. Then you stand up, throw your guns on him, and put him under arrest."

Both men bent low.

Tommy Taubert drew up to a hitching post and pulled rein. Ben Sanders moved out of the deep shadows. From where he stood, he could see the look of agony on the youthful cowboy's face.

Tommy set his eyes on him and said in a weak, broken voice, "Mr. Sanders, I'm in trouble. *Real* trouble. I've come to ask you—"

Young Taubert's words were cut off as both possemen sprang up, leveling their guns on him.

"You're right, boy!" bellowed Clarence Palmer. "You are in a heap of trouble! Now get those hands in the air! You're under arrest!"

Tommy raised his hands and said feebly, "You don't need those guns, Mr. Palmer. Are you and Mr. Nelson part of the posse?"

"Sure are," Palmer affirmed. "Duly sworn in and authorized by the El Paso marshal's office to arrest you for murder." Holding his weapon steady, he said from the side of his mouth, "Get his gun, Ben."

The rancher stepped off the porch and slipped Tommy's revolver from its holster.

"Now get off the horse nice and easy, boy," came Clarence Palmer's sharp command.

Young Taubert gave Ben Sanders a forlorn look and then dismounted slowly. Ignoring Palmer and Nelson, he said, "Mr. Sanders, I came back to—"

"*Tommy!*" shrieked Melinda, bursting out the door and crossing the porch. Tears fell as she threw her arms around him, sobbing, "Oh, Tommy, you came back! I knew you would!" Still clinging to him, she turned to her father and said, "You see, Daddy? He came back! Tommy is no outlaw!"

Young Taubert embraced the woman he loved, unable to speak for the hot lump in his throat. Clinging to her, he wept.

Evelyn Sanders stood on the porch, her own lips quivering.

After several moments, Ben Sanders stepped to his daughter and said, "All right, Melinda, move away now. Tommy has been placed under arrest. These men must handcuff him. They will hold him here until Marshal Langford returns."

Releasing his hold on Melinda, who continued weeping and drawing shaky breaths, Tommy said, "Mr. Sanders, they don't need to shackle me. I came here for the purpose of asking you to ride with me into El Paso so I could turn myself over to the law."

The rancher's face turned to marble. "Likely story. You came back here to see Melinda and ask her to become a fugitive with you. That's what you really came here for, wasn't it? To get her to run away with you!"

"No, sir," said the broken young man. "I came for the reason I just told you. I thought you were my friend. I thought you would let me explain what happened and then go with me to the marshal."

"You're not dealing with some misdemeanor, here, Taubert," spoke up Oscar Nelson. "This is *murder*. What do you expect of Mr. Sanders? He trusted you. He gave you a job. He—"

"Just a minute!" cut in Melinda. "Tommy has asked for a chance to give his side of the story to my father. The least you can do is give him that opportunity."

Giving his daughter a look of disgust, Sanders said, "Okay, let's all go over here on the porch and sit down. I'll listen right now."

The possemen crowded close to their prisoner as the group took chairs. Melinda sat next to her mother, who held her hand.

Facing the rancher, Tommy said, "I never told you about my brother, Mr. Sanders, because I am ashamed of him. He is an outlaw and an ex-convict."

Tommy told of Jack's past, of how he had broken the hearts of their parents, and of the inheritance they had left when they died. He explained about their going into town so Jack could cash the bank draft and gave the details of the subsequent shoot-out.

Finishing his explanation of the shooting, he said, "I am sick about Mr. Bandy being killed, but it all happened so fast. I was pressed into a situation where whatever I did, I was wrong. Now I have to live with the fact that I took another man's life to save my brother's."

"See, Daddy!" cried Melinda. "Tommy is not an outlaw! Somebody has got to help him!"

Sanders raised a hand, signaling her to be quiet. Looking at Tommy in the gloom, he said, "If you weren't in on the robbery, why did you run away?"

"Like I said, sir, it all happened so fast. We were off and galloping out of town before I knew it. We hid out by a cave on the west side of the mountains. Jack went to see a rancher he was supposed to be going to work for. Said he would be back soon and we would head for Tucson. He had promised me before he pulled the holdup that he was going to go straight. I was a fool for believing him."

"Sounds like it," commented the rancher.

"Anyway," continued the broken young cowboy, "the longer I sat there in the cave and pondered the situation, the more I felt the hopelessness of my future. For the rest of my life, I would be on the run. I would always have to live in fear and dread, looking over my shoulder . . . always waiting for some lawman to shove a gun in my back."

Tommy ran his fingers through his ash-blond hair. "I just decided there at the cave, Mr. Sanders, that I would rather die than live like that. So here I am. Guess you won't need to ride to town with me. Mr. Palmer and Mr. Nelson can keep me in custody till the marshal comes."

Clarence Palmer looked at his partner. "I don't think those handcuffs will be necessary, Oscar."

Nelson nodded his agreement.

"There's one other thing I may as well tell you, Mr. Sanders," said Tommy. "And you, too, Mrs. Sanders. Not that anything can ever come out of it . . . but I love your daughter. I love her very, very much. If for no other reason, I *would* have come back to see her. But believe me, sir, I would never have asked her to run away with me. Melinda is a fine and wonderful woman. I would never want to mar her character or hurt her relationship with you."

With gleaming moisture in her eyes, Melinda said, "I may as well tell you also, Daddy, that I love Tommy. I love him with all my heart. I don't know what is going to happen to him, but I am going to stand by him all the way."

"We'll talk about that," said Sanders icily. "No daughter of mine is going to align herself with a criminal."

Tommy's face pinched.

Evelyn Sanders said, "Ben, aren't you being a little harsh? The boy has opened his soul to you. He has come to you for help and understanding."

"I understand, all right," her husband retorted. "I understand that tonight Jim Bandy lies dead on a slab in El Paso. This man who says he loves your daughter murdered him. That's what I understand. And if I understand the law in Texas correctly, Mr. Taubert here is going to hang for his crime."

Melinda felt her heart turn to ice.

* * *

Texas Ranger Branson Howard waited patiently for Ernie Carpenter to come into the barn with the blue roan. He could see moonlight through cracks in the walls and through a dirty window.

Hours passed, and Branson finally decided that something had gone wrong. Somehow, he had to free himself. It was obvious that there was no way Turk Killam could let him live. The Ranger knew he must get loose or die.

In a moment of desperation, he lunged against the rope that held him, testing the strength of the vertical beam to which he was tied. To his surprise, the base of the beam gave slightly. Dust particles showered him from overhead.

Gathering his strength, he lunged again. The beam gave off a splitting sound, and more dust fell.

Branson was sure, now, that he could rip the beam from its rotted mooring. His only worry was the possibility of bringing the hayloft down on top of him. He decided that he had no choice. He would have to take the chance.

The Ranger thought of Hugh Pyle. Whether he was in the house or the bunkhouse, he would hear the noise when the beam came loose. Branson would have to work fast in the darkness to slip the rope over one end of the beam, free himself of the rope, on the blade of one of the scythes he had seen when being brought into the barn, and be ready to meet Pyle when he came through the door.

Thinking it over carefully, he knew that his chances of successfully getting loose and overpowering Pyle would increase a hundred percent if he had some light. He decided to wait until dawn, gambling that the gang would not return in the meantime. Leaning his head back against the beam, he wondered what time it was.

Inside the house, Ernie Carpenter lay on the kitchen floor asleep. His snoring was a loud, wheezing, mournful sound.

Hugh Pyle drank coffee while time passed slowly. His gun lay near his hand. Lucy sat quietly across the table from him, trying to stay awake. Finally, the grandfather clock in the front room rang five times.

Pyle swore, shifting positions on the chair. "Turk and the boys should've been back by now," he complained. "Another few minutes, it'll be dawn."

Lucy did not comment. Throwing her gaze toward the living room door, she said, "I think Mother is awake." Quickly, she stood up.

Pyle grabbed his gun, eyeing her warily. "Where you going?"

"I said I think Mother is awake. I'm going to check on her."

"Don't you pull anything funny, like trying to go to the barn."

Giving the outlaw a disgusted look, she left and went to her mother's bed. In the dim light, she saw that Dorothy was indeed awake.

"Mother," she said, "what are you doing awake at this hour?"

"I haven't been able to sleep, honey," responded Dorothy.

"You're crying," Lucy said, taking hold of her hand. "What's the matter?"

"Honey," sniffed her mother, speaking low, "I can't stand seeing you in this situation any longer. Things are getting worse around here, and Turk is getting meaner. Please, Lucy, get away while you can. That Texas Ranger, he'll help you. Tell Ernie to handle Hugh. Go out there and let that Ranger loose. Go, Lucy. Please!"

"No, Mother, I can't," breathed Lucy. "I can't leave you. I *won't* leave you. I'm staying right here with you as long as you live."

"But, honey," pleaded Dorothy, "it isn't fair. It isn't—"

Suddenly, there was a loud, thundering noise at the barn. Gun in hand, Hugh Pyle ran past the two women and charged out the door.

Lucy ran into the kitchen and began shaking Ernie, attempting to awaken him.

At the barn, Hugh Pyle cocked his revolver and flung open the big squeaky door. The interior was dark, but he could make out the outline of the sagging hayloft. The spot where Branson had been tied was a mass of broken timber.

"Okay, Ranger!" Pyle shouted. "Come on out!"

Only silence greeted him.

"Hey!" bellowed the outlaw. "I said come out!"

The barn was like a tomb.

Squinting against the gray gloom, Pyle studied the pile of boards where the loft had collapsed. "Wait a minute," he muttered. "Maybe you can't come out. Maybe you outfoxed yourself. Ha! Hey, Ranger, did you bury yourself?"

The outlaw's curiosity was yearning to be satisfied. Holding the revolver poised for action, he eased his way through the door. Moving slowly, he tiptoed toward the rubble. He was nearly there when a rustling sound met his ears. He turned just in time to see the board coming for his head in a full arc.

Pyle made a partial turn, lowering his head, and the board struck his shoulder. The outlaw stumbled off balance from the blow but swung the gun and fired. The bullet narrowly missed Branson's head. Responding quickly, he stepped in and kicked Pyle's gun hand savagely. The weapon sailed into a pile of straw and disappeared. Pyle made a dive for it, clawing frantically at the straw.

Branson looked around quickly in the gathering light. There was a pitchfork leaning against a stall within his reach. He grasped it and turned back to see Pyle bringing the deadly muzzle up, his eyes wild.

Branson reacted lightning fast. Leaping forward, he plunged the tines into Pyle's throat in one savage, fluid movement. The outlaw made a gagging sound as blood bubbled around the holes. His eyes bulged with horror, and the gun slid from his fingers. He gave a piteous whine and slumped against the tines in death.

The Ranger leaned over and picked up the revolver. As he straightened up, Lucy Daniels appeared at the door. She looked at Branson, then the dead man, then Branson again. "Oh, Branson!" she blurted, dashing to him.

Dorothy Killam had watched Hugh Pyle dash out the door when the loud, rumbling noise came from the barn. Thumbing tears from her eyes, she had listened as Lucy ran into the kitchen and began calling Ernie's name.

Dorothy knew that the big man was very difficult to rouse from sleep. Lucy had yelled in his ears, shaking his head, but Ernie had slept on. Then a gunshot had been heard, and Lucy had left Ernie and dashed out the door.

Now Dorothy Killam listened intently until she was certain Ernie was still asleep. She knew this was her only opportunity.

With concentrated effort, the despairing woman raised up on her elbows and pulled herself toward the edge of the bed. Her lifeless legs trailed as if they were logs that were tied to her body. Laying her head back for a moment, she gathered her strength, saying, "I will set you free, Lucy."

Raising up again, Dorothy inched herself over the edge. Teetering for a moment, she said, "Forgive me, God," and plummeted downward.

Branson Howard held Lucy in his arms for several minutes. Then she said, "Branson, you must get away from here fast. Turk and the others will be back anytime now. They will kill you."

"All right," he replied. "I'll go. But I'll be back with help. Soon this nightmare will be over for you."

Lucy and Branson reached the door. He was breaking away from her to head for the corral when they both saw the massive form of Ernie Carpenter on the porch of the house. He was rubbing his eyes and calling to Lucy.

"What is it, Ernie?" she called back.

"Your mother, Miss Lucy," he said calmly. "She is asleep on the floor."

Tommy Taubert stood facing Marshal Bart Langford in the yard of the Sanders home. In spite of her father's disapproval, Melinda stood next to Tommy, her golden hair shining in the morning sun.

Young Taubert told the complete story to the marshal and the posse. As he finished, Payton Roads spoke up. "I believe the boy, Marshal. I think it is just like he told it. Tommy had no idea his brother was going to pull a holdup. I remember seeing the look on Tommy's face when he saw what Jack was doing. It shocked him. I have no doubt he was innocent."

"Thank you, Mr. Roads." Melinda smiled. "It's about time somebody around here was saying something in Tommy's behalf." Her flinty eyes swerved to her father.

Ben Sanders adjusted himself uncomfortably under Melinda's hot gaze.

Marshal Langford hitched the gun belt up below his ample belly and said, "I believe Tommy's story, Miss Melinda. However, that does not erase the fact that he shot and killed Jim Bandy. He will have to stand trial for murder."

"I guess it means nothing that I was going to turn myself in," said young Taubert weakly.

"That depends, son," Langford replied. "Your coming here is no real proof that you were going to do that. I, for one, believe you. Maybe the jurors will believe you. Maybe they won't. Even if they do, it may not save you from the gallows."

A cold, hard lump settled in Melinda's stomach. Clinging to Tommy, she broke into tears. "Oh, Marshal!" she sobbed. "They can't hang him! They just can't hang him!"

"Let's go, son," said the lawman.

Evelyn folded Melinda into her arms as Tommy Taubert was torn from her and ushered to his horse.

Langford settled into his saddle and turned to the rancher. "See you later, Ben."

Sanders nodded silently.

Twisting in his saddle, Tommy said, "I'm sorry to be a disappointment to you, Mr. Sanders. I wish it were me that was dead instead of the barber." Then setting his gaze on Melinda, he choked out the words, "I love you."

Through burning tears, Melinda watched the posse ride away with their prisoner.

Chapter Fourteen

The sun was lifting high into the morning sky when the posse and their prisoner, Tommy Taubert, turned through the gate marked with Turk Killam's name and approached the ranch where Tommy had told them his brother might be found. Marshal Langford gave directions for his men to fan out and ride toward the house and outbuildings from different directions. Jack Taubert must be caught.

As they closed in moments later, it was immediately apparent that the place was deserted. The house was standing open, with no one inside. Payton Roads and two other men rode over to look inside the barn, which also stood open.

Marshal Langford and the others were discussing the situation when Roads appeared at the barn door, calling, "Bart! We've got a dead man in here!"

Leaving Tommy Taubert with the rest of the posse, Langford entered the barn and set his eyes on the cold, stiff body of Hugh Pyle. The pitchfork was still buried in his throat. His glasslike eyes were wide open, frozen in a look of horror.

"Pull the fork out, Payton," Langford said, turning away from the gory sight. "I'll send the undertaker out for the body. The men are tired. We'll take up the chase on Jack Taubert later."

Mounting again, the marshal said, "Tommy, it seems like wherever your brother goes, men turn up dead. Have you got any idea where he might be now?"

"He might have gone back to the cave. We could

swing by there on the way to town. It's not much out of the way."

Turk Killam swore vehemently as he and his two men walked gingerly across the desert. He would find Jack Taubert if it was the last thing he ever did.

Slowly, the barefoot men picked their way in the direction of the ranch, wincing, cursing, and complaining. Their feet were bleeding and beginning to swell.

"What are you gonna do with that Ranger, Turk?" asked Al Weems.

"As I see it," replied Killam, "there ain't but one choice. I'm gonna kill him. But the first one to die when we get home is that big lamebrain. Now that Bill's dead, I don't plan to put up with Ernie anymore. It's gonna be a real pleasure to put a bullet in his head."

"Lucy will holler her head off over that," put in Dirk Holstead. "And killing the Ranger, too."

"So let her holler," growled Killam. "She'll get over it."

"Hey, boss," said Weems, stopping in his tracks and pointing northwest. "There's a bunch of riders coming."

All three outlaws peered through the heat waves that were dancing in the distance.

"Posse!" gasped Holstead.

"Turk, if they've been to the ranch," said Weems, "they know that we stole the gold. That Ranger has told them everything! We're cooked!"

"Shut up!" snarled Killam. "Maybe they're just returning to El Paso. Might even have Taubert's brother in custody. Let's don't panic."

"But El Paso's due south," argued Weems. "Why are they angling in this direction, unless they're coming after us?"

"I said don't panic," rumbled Killam. "Maybe there's no problem. Let's just stand here and wait. We sure can't run from them."

"What are we going to tell them, boss?" asked

Holstead, trying to remain calm. "I mean, about why we're in this fix. And what are we going to do if they offer to take us to the ranch? It would be mighty easy for them to find out that Ranger is tied up in the barn."

Killam wiped a shaky hand over his sweaty brow. "I don't know what to do *or* say," he answered with short, clipped words. "Just let me handle it. I'll think of something."

The sound of hooves and creaking leather met the ears of the three sore-footed outlaws as the posse drew near.

"Turk, I don't like this!" whispered Weems from the side of his mouth.

"Shut up!" snapped Killam.

Bart Langford signaled for the riders with him to halt. As they did, he eyed the barefoot men. Knowing from Tommy that his brother had been at the Killam ranch, he said, "Jack Taubert take your boots, Turk?"

The outlaws did not notice Langford's prisoner— Tommy was just a face among many in the posse—so they assumed that the posse had been at the ranch and been told everything.

While Killam was trying to think of what to say, Langford unwittingly added to their rising fear by speaking solemnly, "We just came from your ranch, Turk. There's a dead man in your barn."

Panic shot through Killam. He immediately assumed that Hugh Pyle had killed the Texas Ranger and that Pyle, or Lucy, had told Langford about Jack Taubert joining the gang and about the gold heist.

Killam's mind froze with fear. He could think only of steering clear of the murder charge. He blurted out, "I told Pyle not to kill that Ranger, Marshal! I swear it! Didn't I, Al? Dirk? Okay, we stole the gold, but you know we didn't kill Rainey and those Pinkerton guards! No, sir! I ain't no killer, Marshal. We just tied them up. And . . . and . . . we don't even have the gold anymore. That damned Jack Taubert took it from us!"

Langford quickly put two and two together. Somehow Turk Killam or Jack Taubert had learned of the gold that Captain Branson Howard and the three Pinkerton men were going to transport to Austin. Apparently they had forced Frank Rainey to open the vault and then taken off with the gold, leaving him and the others bound. Jack Taubert had then gotten the drop on Killam and his men and had left with the gold and their horses, boots, and guns.

Settling back in his saddle and looking down at the cowering three, Langford said, "This gold robbery is news to me. I appreciate your willing confession, Turk."

Dirk Holstead turned on Killam, his eyes round and naked with frenzy. "Turk, you *fool!*" he exclaimed. "You just convicted us! You told Al and me not to panic, and you did it yourself!"

Al Weems turned pale, a veil of despair covering his eyes.

Shifting on his bleeding feet, Killam looked at the lawman with unbelieving eyes. His ruddy features were creased by deep, jagged lines. He suddenly looked twenty years older. He spoke in a voice thick and almost unreal to himself. "Marshal, are . . . are you telling me that . . . that you haven't heard about the gold robbery?"

"Nope. We haven't been back to town since we left yesterday morning."

"So it's because of the dead Ranger that you're coming after me?"

Langford slid from his saddle. When his feet touched earth, he said, "Nope. I don't know about any dead Ranger."

Killam's heavy jaw slacked. "But you said the Ranger in my barn is dead."

Langford grinned sardonically. "I never said anything about a Ranger, Turk. That was your conscience talking. All I said was that there was a dead *man* in your barn." He pushed and then asked, "This Ranger you're talking about . . . His name Howard? Branson Howard?"

"Yeah." Killam nodded.

"I know him," said the marshal. "He's definitely not the dead man in your barn. This man was short, stocky, wore long, curly sideburns, and had the initials H.P. in his hat."

Killam was dumbfounded when he realized that Hugh Pyle was dead. He was even more befuddled when Langford told him that there was no one at the ranch. *Not even Dorothy.*

Totally defeated, Killam, Weems, and Holstead surrendered to Langford and the posse. Killam then told the marshal about Bill Storey's body at the cave. The outlaws rode double with the possemen as they returned to the cave and picked up Storey's body. With the body draped over one of the horses, the posse, along with prisoners Killam, Weems, Holstead, and Tommy Taubert, rode for El Paso in the blistering heat of the relentless sun.

Out on the desert twenty miles west of the cave, Jack Taubert gathered all the canteens on his saddle and then released the string of horses, except for the one he was riding and the one he was using as a packhorse. He pressed on, with the horse bearing the two hundred pounds of nuggets trailing him on a lead rope. With little mercy for the animal under him or the one following, he pushed hard toward Tucson, only occasionally taking a swallow from a canteen and grudgingly watering the animals from the same source. The sun's heat was like a blast furnace.

Jack's lifelong dream had been fulfilled. He was suddenly a very wealthy man. Ahead lay Tucson, with its saloons, women, and gambling tables. Beyond Tucson was San Francisco, where he would live a life of luxury.

The ex-convict was so overjoyed with his riches and so eager to close the gap between himself and Tucson that he kept the sweating animals at a steady trot.

"C'mon, you lazy meatheads!" Jack shouted at the panting beasts.

Suddenly the horse he was riding stepped in a hole and went down hard, dislodging him from the saddle. He sailed through the air, rolling into a patch of prickly pear cactus. Screaming in pain, he jumped up and stood over the fallen horse. Its leg was broken severely, and it was nickering with pain.

Swearing profusely, he took his canteen and saddle-bags and mounted the packhorse, leaving the frightened, hurting animal in its helpless condition. Delirious with his wealth and eager to spend some of it, he pushed the heavily laden animal westward.

Lucy Daniels clung to Branson Howard as El Paso's undertaker and his assistant carried her mother's body into the back room of the funeral parlor. Her eyes were swollen from weeping.

Returning to the front office, the undertaker discussed burial details with her. Dorothy Killam's body would be laid to rest at ten o'clock the next morning.

The couple returned to the sun-struck street and climbed into the wagon next to Ernie Carpenter. Branson saw the worship in the big man's eyes as he looked at Lucy and said, "Please don't be sad, Miss Lucy. I will take care of you. Don't be afraid."

The lovely brunette patted his hand. "Thank you, Ernie," she said softly. "I'm not afraid."

"Maybe Miss Dorothy will wake up and come home tomorrow," Ernie said slowly.

Branson smiled at the big man's simplicity, admiring the tender devotion he held for Lucy Daniels.

"We wouldn't want her to wake up unless she could be well and walk like other people, would we, Ernie?" Lucy said in response to his words of optimism.

"No, ma'am," he replied.

Branson took her hand. Looking up at him, she pressed a smile to her lips.

"I love you," he said softly. Looking past Lucy, he told Ernie to drive the wagon to the marshal's office.

While the wagon rolled up the street, Lucy spoke in a melancholy manner. "She did it for me, Branson. She knew I would never leave the ranch unless she was dead."

"Your mother was a mighty fine woman, Lucy," he replied.

"I meant what I said to Ernie. I wouldn't wish her back to have the miserable existence that she's known for the past six years."

The wagon ground to a halt in front of the marshal's office. The door was closed and the blinds drawn. Two elderly men sat in the shade near the door. Looking at them, Branson asked, "Marshal and the posse haven't returned yet?"

"Not yet," one of the men replied, spewing a brown stream across the board sidewalk into the street.

Turning to Lucy, Branson said, "We'll get you and Ernie each a hotel room where you can stay until Killam and the gang are arrested. Then we'll—"

The Ranger's words were cut off by the sight of a group of riders coming up San Francisco Street from the west. The posse had returned.

People were coming off the boardwalk, shouting to Marshal Langford about the gold robbery. They were surprised to hear him say that three of the men he had in custody were in the gang that took the gold. He pointed out Turk Killam as the gang's leader.

Someone asked, "Did you get the gold back, Marshal?"

"No," answered Langford reluctantly, "but we will. There's only one gang member still at large. He has the gold. I'll take a couple of men and go after him soon as we rest up a bit."

Another suddenly recognized Tommy Taubert. Pointing at him, he said, "Hey, Bart! You got one of the killers!"

Tommy dipped his chin in shame.

"Hey, everybody!" shouted the same man, walking beside the procession, "we're gonna have us a hanging!"

A few in the gathering crowd cheered, and Tommy felt a shiver in his spine.

Branson climbed out of the wagon and helped Lucy down as the posse and prisoners reined in. Ernie climbed down beside them.

"Looks like your stepfather will no longer present you a problem," Branson said to Lucy.

"I wonder how he caught them so quickly," Lucy mused, staring at Killam, Weems, and Holstead.

"Must've been pretty easy," Branson said idly. "It's hard to run through rocks and cactus in your bare feet."

Lucy's eyes focused on the bloody, swollen feet of the three outlaws. "Oh, my goodness!" she gasped.

Turk Killam's gaze met Lucy's. His face was stolid, his dark eyes grim, as he and his men dismounted.

"Hey, Marshal!" shouted someone in the crowd. "How come you don't have those criminals in handcuffs?"

Annoyed by the question, Langford said, "Take a look at their feet. They aren't going anywhere."

Sighting the Texas Ranger, the marshal called out, "Ah, there you are, Branson. I understand you were at the Killam ranch. You the one that speared that hombre with the pitchfork?"

"I see you've been there yourself," Branson replied. "I came in to tell you about the dead outlaw and to put you onto Killam's trail. Guess you don't need my information."

The lawman snickered. "Guess not."

"Did I understand you to say only one of the gang got away?"

"Yep. Jack Taubert. Seems yesterday was a busy day for him. He took off with the gold and these fellas' boots. Even killed one of them by the name of Bill Storey."

Ernie Carpenter's head came up. His dull eyes sharpened at the sound of his cousin's name as Langford and Branson proceeded with their discussion.

"Is Cousin Bill here?" Ernie asked.

Langford paid Ernie no mind as he began to grope about, looking for his cousin.

Nearby, Killam spoke to Oscar Nelson, who was guarding him. "That's my daughter over there. Can I talk to her?"

"You'll have to make it quick," Nelson replied. He

escorted the limping outlaw leader toward the spot where Lucy stood with Branson Howard.

Killam threw the Texas Ranger a mean look as he came up to Lucy. Swinging his gaze on her, he said, "Where's your mother?"

"She's dead," Lucy replied coldly. "Rolled herself off the bed. Snapped her spine."

While Lucy was talking to Killam, Ernie found the body of Bill Storey draped over the horse at the rear of the procession. Sinking his thick fingers into Storey's hair, he pulled the ashen face upward. Some of the onlookers took pity on him as they saw the bewildered look in his eyes and heard him say, "Wake up, Cousin Bill. We need to go home. Miss Dorothy will be there. She can walk like you and me now."

Perplexed by his cousin's failure to respond, Ernie thumbed open one eye. Bending to look into the eye, he said, "See, Cousin Bill, it's me. Can we go home, now? You can ride in the wagon with me and Miss Lucy."

At the same moment, Turk Killam was listening to his stepdaughter explain the burial arrangements. While Lucy talked, Killam's mind was working. Oscar Nelson's attention was focused on the marshal's conversation with Branson Howard. His holstered gun was within arm's reach of Killam's left hand. Also within arm's reach was the dark-eyed brunette.

Killam knew this was his chance. He wished for boots on his feet, but free and barefoot was better than behind bars with new boots on. In one swift move, the bearded outlaw yanked Nelson's revolver from its holster and seized Lucy. Throwing back the hammer, he locked Lucy's neck in the crook of his arm and pressed the muzzle to her head.

The sudden, violent move shocked Lucy, and she cried out. Langford and Branson spun around, and their faces blanched at the sight of Lucy with the gun at her head. At the rear of the string of horses, Ernie Carpenter raised his head at the sound of Lucy's voice.

"Don't anybody move!" boomed Killam. "Me and the

girl are riding out of here!" Backing toward a horse and dragging Lucy along, he said threateningly, "If I see a hand move, I'll blow her pretty head off! Anybody follows, she dies. I mean it!"

Lucy whimpered as Killam neared the horse he had chosen for his escape.

Branson Howard shouted in rage, "Killam! I'll hunt you down like a rabid dog!"

Suddenly all eyes swung to the towering giant, who plodded into the open circle around the bearded outlaw and his beautiful hostage. Ernie Carpenter resembled a massive beast whose mate had been endangered. A dark cloud formed on his normally expressionless face. There was murder in his droopy eyes.

In his slow, thick-tongued manner, Ernie said, "You promised never to touch Miss Lucy no more. Let her loose." As he spoke, he shuffled forward. The onlookers watched with bated breath.

"Tell him to get back, Lucy!" blared Killam. "I'll kill him, and you, too!"

The muzzle hurt Lucy's head as Turk pressed the gun hard against it.

"Ernie!" wailed the frightened young woman. "Stop! Don't come any closer! He'll kill you!"

Like a slow-moving locomotive, the massive man kept coming. "Let her loose," he grumbled.

The crowd was spellbound by the scene before them. Branson wanted to charge in but did not dare as long as the muzzle was pressed to Lucy's head.

Killam's features were twisted in a combination of fear and wrath. Heavy black brows hooded his wild, insane eyes. "I'll kill you!" he exploded.

"No, Ernie!" shrieked Lucy. "Stop!"

Ernie kept coming.

Killam swung the muzzle from Lucy's head, lined it on the big man's broad chest, and dropped the hammer. The gun roared. Ernie winced as the .44 caliber slug tore into his body, but he kept coming.

Lucy screamed, and Killam fired again.

Ernie hesitated, twitching as the second bullet struck

him, and then he shuffled on toward Killam with grim
determination. Killam's attention was focused on the
menacing giant. He didn't see Branson Howard coming
at him from the side. Tommy Taubert was also in
motion.

Ernie closed in like a wounded grizzly, facing the
fiery breath of the gun as it exploded a third time. He
grunted and reached out with both hands as Killam
thumbed back the hammer again.

Abruptly, Branson snatched Lucy from Killam's grasp.
At the same instant, Tommy seized the gun, wrenching
it from the frightened outlaw's hand.

Ernie gripped Killam, who yelled with terror, his
eyes wild. Methodically, the big angry man closed Killam
in a bear hug, lifting him off the ground.

The crowd was mesmerized, unable to tear their eyes
from the dramatic spectacle.

Gritting his teeth, Ernie growled, "You promised
you would never hurt Miss Lucy no more. You lied!"
His powerful arms bore down fiercely. Bones popped
and cracked.

Turk Killam let loose an ear-piercing, primal scream.
The clapboard buildings along San Francisco Street
echoed his torment as the crowd watched in horror.
The look of death was in the outlaw's bulging eyes.

Ernie bore down harder, grinding his teeth. Bones
snapped. Killam's face was purple.

Blood began to flow from Ernie's mouth. He growled
wildly, giving his arms a savage jerk, and Killam's spine
snapped like a dry twig. His body seemed to cave in.
He coughed once and sagged against his massive
conqueror.

Breathing heavily, Ernie let Killam's limp, loose-
jointed corpse fall to the ground like a discarded rag
doll. He stood swaying like a tall tree in a high wind.

"*Ernie!*" Lucy screamed.

The huge man keeled over and hit the street hard.

Instantly, Lucy Daniels was kneeling at his side.
Three rings of blood were evident on the bib of his
overalls, each spreading rapidly.

Branson Howard quickly flanked the weeping young woman. Tears burned her eyes as she peered into the fallen giant's pallid face.

Ernie Carpenter looked up at Lucy with fondness in his bleary eyes. He licked his lips and spoke through the bloody froth, forcing a weak smile. "Miss Lucy, I fixed him so he won't hurt you no more."

The big man's eyes rolled back. "I love you," he whispered. Then his droopy lids went shut and he released his last breath.

"I love you, too," Lucy whimpered as she tenderly stroked the giant's boyish face, so still now in death. Tears dripped from her chin, mingling with the blood on Ernie's unmoving breast.

Chapter Fifteen

Jack Taubert swore as he drained the last drop of water from his last canteen. Straining his red-rimmed eyes against the blinding glare of the bleak, burning desert, he looked westward. How far away was Tucson?

The heat had taken its toll on his reasoning powers. The outlaw could not remember how long he had been traveling with his two hundred pounds of shiny nuggets. Had he spent a night since leaving Killam and the others at the cave? He decided he had. Maybe two. Tucson was probably just over that range of mountains in the distance. Another day would put him there.

Man and beast felt the increasing drive of the fierce heat as the sun rose higher in the empty sky. The horse's ears lopped forward, its dry mouth sagged, and its head drooped.

Looking around him, Jack felt the desert mocking him. Shaking his fist at the sun, he said defiantly, "You won't get me, old boy! Jack Taubert is rich, do you hear me? Rich! Me and my gold, we're going to make it to Tucson. We're getting close now. We're gonna make it!"

Pushing the panting horse across the blistering sand, the outlaw muttered, "I'm a rich man, a very rich man. Just a little way to Tucson."

The rich man did not realize he had traveled less than one hundred miles. There were still over two hundred miles between him and Tucson.

* * *

Lucy Daniels stood at the window of her room in the Rio Grande Hotel, looking down on the street below. Branson Howard had checked her into the room and kissed her gently. He had just left, telling her to get some rest. He was going with Marshal Langford to arrest Henry Yates and would return soon.

Branson's tenderness and concern was a genuine solace to Lucy in the loss of her mother and Ernie Carpenter. She and the handsome man were little more than strangers, but she knew she was very much in love.

The Ranger now appeared on the street, looking up and waving at her. She blew him a kiss. He returned it and then gave the blue roan a pat on the rump, leaving it tied at the hitch rail in front of the hotel. He would walk to the marshal's office.

Lucy watched until Branson passed from view and then gazed up the street, staying at the window to catch the merciful breeze that was stirring. While idly observing the active street below, she reflected on her mother's supreme sacrifice to free her from Turk Killam. *Ironic*, she thought. *Turk is dead, now. I'm free anyway.*

And then there was poor Ernie Carpenter. His devotion to Lucy had cost him his life.

Lucy saw Dr. Finch's buggy pass down the street. Only seconds later, she noticed a rough-looking man ride up to the hitch rail in front of the hotel and dismount. He seemed to be interested in Branson's blue roan. After looking the roan over for a moment, the man crossed the street. Lucy saw the way he walked and recognized the familiar carriage of a gunfighter, which was confirmed by the gun slung low on his hip and thonged to his thigh. When he sat down on a bench in the shade in front of the Little Sombrero Café across the street, she turned her attention elsewhere.

At El Paso's jail, Tommy Taubert sat glumly in his cell. His whole life was shattered, and now he faced the gallows. All of this was because of his shiftless, no-good brother.

Tommy's heart yearned for Melinda. She was the

only good thing that had ever happened to him. And now he would lose her, too, when he took the drop to the end of the hangman's rope.

Young Taubert watched as Marshal Langford and Branson Howard brought in Henry Yates and locked him in a cell. Yates glared hotly through the bars at Al Weems and Dirk Holstead, who were in the cell next to him.

With Branson standing at his side, the marshal stood in front of Taubert's cell and said, "I'll be going after your brother tomorrow, Tommy. With the load he's dragging, I should be able to catch him within two or three days." Nodding toward Branson, he added, "I'm going to try to talk the Ranger, here, into pursuing him with me."

Branson said with a smile, "I've been wanting to discuss that with you, Bart. Let's go into the office and—"

The Ranger was interrupted by a man bursting through the door. "Marshal!" he exclaimed. "There's a drunken cowboy over at the Broken Horseshoe. He's waving a broken whiskey bottle around, threatening to cut somebody's face! You better come!"

Langford sighed. "See you later," he said to Branson and was gone.

Branson left the jail. He would take the roan to the livery and then check on Lucy.

Moments later, the broad-shouldered Ranger stepped between the roan and another horse and loosed the reins from the rail. "Come on, boy," he said, fluffing the animal's long mane, "let's take you to your hotel."

Suddenly a cold voice from the middle of the street barked, "Hey! You with the roan!"

From her window on the hotel's second floor, Lucy Daniels had been watching Branson from behind the sheer curtains. The sun was now slanting its rays through the window as she saw the man she loved turn to face the gunfighter.

Setting his unflinching eyes on the man who was addressing him, Branson said levelly, "You talking to me?"

"Where'd you get that roan?" came the sharp demand.

The Ranger knew immediately who he was facing—Vic Barry. The outlaw must have been to the oasis and found the bodies of his two partners, along with those of the two horses.

"That's none of your business," Branson retorted, lowering his gun belt a few inches. The holster was not tied down. It could slow his draw, but there was no way to correct it now.

"You stole that horse, mister," Barry said accusingly. "That is, *after* you murdered its owner and his partner. They were my friends."

"You've got it wrong, fella," parried the Ranger. "Your friends tried to murder me. As you can see, they were unsuccessful. But they shot my horse, so I took the roan. That's it, plain and simple. Now get off my back."

Stepping closer, the gun hawk said, "You're talking to Vic Barry, big mouth. Do you realize that?"

"Never heard the name," Branson said icily, not allowing Barry any satisfaction, though the gunman's reputation was well known. "Am I suppose to tremble?"

A swollen, dangerous look filled Vic Barry's wicked eyes. "You're gonna draw against me, mister!"

Moving away from the roan and stepping into the street, Branson said, "I've been planning on that ever since you first hollered at me."

Vic Barry could wait no longer. His hand snaked toward his gun.

The Ranger's hand was a colorless blur. His gun belched fire. Vic Barry took the slug square in the heart, his own weapon barely clearing leather. He fell backward with one leg twisted grotesquely beneath him.

Smoke was still in the air when Branson felt Lucy's arms go around him. Holstering his weapon, he held her close.

Marshal Langford arrived on the scene, and bystanders quickly told him the facts. He ordered Barry's body removed from the street and then approached Branson, who still held Lucy in his arms.

"Rangers must need to be fast," chuckled Langford. "You took out one of the fastest just now, and your holster isn't even tied down."

"Comes with the territory," Branson said blandly.

"How about dinner?" asked the marshal. "We'll talk about going after Jack Taubert."

"An hour from now all right?" responded Branson.

Langford agreed, and they decided to meet at the Little Sombrero.

Branson escorted Lucy back to her room so she could freshen up for dinner. As they stepped inside, he took her in his arms and looked into her tired eyes. "It's been a pretty rough day for you, hasn't it?"

Lucy nodded quietly.

"I have to ask you something."

"Yes?"

"Would . . . would it make any difference how you felt about me if you knew I used to be a . . . a . . ."

"Gunfighter?" she finished for him. "Not in the least, darling. I've known that since the first time I saw you."

"Really? How?"

"Gunfighters have a certain way they carry themselves. Because of Turk Killam, I was around them a lot." Slipping her arms about his neck, she flipped off his hat and buried her fingers in the thick mane at the back of his head. Looking deep into his eyes, she said, "It makes no difference to me what you were. It's what you *are* that counts."

Lucy pulled his head down and touched him with her soft, velvet lips.

Holding her head against his chest, Branson said, "With Turk dead, you're free, Lucy. But I don't like it."

Pulling her head back, she gave him a perplexed look and said, "You don't want me to be free?"

"Not completely," he replied flatly.

"Why not?"

"Because you are too beautiful to be running around free. You need to be attached."

"Oh, I do?" Lucy said, arching her eyebrows. "To whom?"

"To me." Branson smiled, his teeth gleaming beneath his dark mustache. "Will you marry me?"

"Let me think it over," she said, touching her fingertips to her temples and looking down. Within three seconds, she looked up and said, "Yes!"

The sun turned to crimson as it touched the mountains on the western horizon, losing some of its heat.

Jack Taubert's throat was like clotted dust. A dry, white froth ringed his mouth. He looked thinner than ever, and his eyes were bloodshot and bleary. The mountains still seemed so far away. Discouragement began to claim him, but the thought of his riches renewed his vigor. He told himself the desert haze made the mountains appear to be farther away than they actually were.

Just as the sun disappeared behind the saw-toothed range, the horse's legs buckled and it went down, raising puffs of dust. Leaping from the saddle, Jack swore at the exhausted, dehydrated animal. Lashing its face with the reins, he screamed, "Get up! We're almost there! C'mon, I said, get up!"

Blinking against the stinging leathers, the frightened beast lifted itself and the two hundred pounds of dead weight and stood up. "That's more like it," Jack said, swinging back into the saddle. "We'll keep moving till it gets dark."

The desert sky was turning purple when the horse went down again. "Okay, okay," Jack said to the gasping animal. "We'll rest here for a while."

Removing the eight canvas bags, he forced the horse onto its feet again and then removed the saddle. He tied the animal to a creosote bush.

Kneeling in the warm sand, Jack opened one of the bags and fondled the shiny nuggets. When it got too dark to see them, he replaced them in the bag and tied it securely. Lying down on the ground and gathering all eight canvas bags around his body, he dropped off to sleep.

It was dark when Jack awakened less than an hour later, yet in his dazed mind he was convinced he had slept through the night and that it was almost dawn. He was determined that by sunset he would be in Tucson. Patting the canvas bags with affection, he rose to his feet, the thirst once again making itself known. It was then that he saw the dead horse lying stretched out on the ground.

Jack cursed everything in sight. He was furious at the thought of leaving any of the gold behind. Then laughing to himself, he said, "Hey, Jack, don't panic! Bury half of it here. Take the other half to Tucson and buy a team and a wagon. Come back and get the rest of it. Thirty thousand is plenty enough to start living high on. Even with that much, you're filthy rich!"

Quickly, the thirst-crazed outlaw dug a shallow hole in the sand with his hands and buried four bags. Shouldering the one hundred pounds of the other four bags, he stumbled westward in the darkness.

The lanterns had been lit along the streets of El Paso as Branson Howard and Lucy Daniels sat down to dinner with Marshal Bart Langford.

As they started eating, Langford said, "I figure if we light out of here right after I take Tommy Taubert before Judge Wilkins for arraignment in the morning, we can still cover a lot of territory tomorrow. I'll have the kid with me at nine when Wilkins opens his office. I should be ready to leave by nine-thirty."

Before Branson had a chance to speak, Dr. Aaron Finch appeared beside the table. "Good evening," he said with a smile.

"Good evening, Doc," replied the marshal. Gesturing toward the one empty chair, he said, "Sit down and join us. You've met these two people, I believe."

"Yes." The physician nodded, giving Lucy and Branson a friendly smile. "How's your head, ma'am?"

Lucy assured him that she was just fine.

When the waitress came, Dr. Finch ordered coffee, which she poured him and then departed.

Conversation at the table covered the recent events, coming ultimately to the young man who faced a murder charge.

"I know Tommy was totally innocent in it all," the marshal said with conviction. "When he shot Jim Bandy, he was only doing what any of us would have done."

"I agree." The Ranger nodded. "I'm sure if I'd been put in the same spot, I would have saved my brother's life, just like he did." Sipping coffee, he added, "The kid is the kind to jump in and help when he sees the need. Just like yesterday. He could have taken a bullet when he went after Turk Killam's gun, but it didn't stop him from doing it."

Langford sighed. "Sure is too bad he has to face a murder charge."

Finch eyed him quizzically. "I thought the only one the kid shot was Bandy."

"It was," said Langford.

"Bandy isn't dead."

The marshal's face stretched tight. "What?"

"I said Bandy isn't dead," came Finch's flat words. "He's home recuperating under his wife's care. He's going to be all right."

"Doc, I don't understand," said Langford, his pulse quickening. "Before I left town with the posse, somebody on the street told me Jim had died."

"I heard it right there in your office, Doctor," spoke up Branson. "I heard someone tell you Jim was dead."

"Oh!" exclaimed Doc. "He was talking about Jim Ebert. Both of them's name is Jim. Must have been the same misunderstanding out on the street where Bart got his information."

"Then that boy won't face a murder charge?" asked Lucy.

"No!" gasped Langford, jumping to his feet. "I've got to tell Tommy about it! I'll be back in a few minutes to discuss hunting down Jack Taubert."

The marshal was elated as he ran up the dusty street. Nearing his office, he saw a golden-haired young woman pacing back and forth in front of the door. Her lathered horse was tied to the hitch rail.

Melinda Sanders's eyes lit up when she spotted the lawman. "Marshal Langford," she said nervously, "I know it's terribly late, but I've been here for a half hour. I want to see Tommy Taubert."

"So do I," he puffed, pulling a key from his pocket.

Langford's shaky hand was fumbling with the lock when a rider thundered up the street and skidded his mount to a halt beside Melinda's horse. It was Ben Sanders.

Melinda's face lost color as he leaped from the saddle, calling her name. Langford swung the office door open and then pivoted, setting his eyes on the irate father.

"Melinda!" blustered Sanders angrily. "What is the meaning of this? Your mother went to your room at suppertime and found the note you left. Get on your horse. We're going home right now."

"Daddy, I meant what I wrote in that note," said Melinda with a trembling voice. "I love Tommy. He needs me!"

Grasping her arm, Sanders rasped, "You'll soon forget Tommy if you just stay away from him. Now let's go."

"I *won't* forget him, Daddy!" she cried, breaking into tears. "I love him!"

"Melinda, listen to me! You can't let yourself get involved any deeper with that killer!"

"Tommy is not a killer, Ben," cut in Langford.

The marshal's husky voice pulled the rancher's head around. "What did you say?"

Melinda wiped away her tears, her eyes wide. "What did you say, Marshal?"

"I just got some mighty good news," Langford said excitedly. "You two come in and hear it while I tell Tommy."

Young Taubert sprang from his bunk when he saw Melinda enter the cell area ahead of the marshal. Quickly, she dashed to him, and they joined hands through the bars. Tommy's countenance fell when he saw the stone-faced rancher enter on Langford's heels. From the nearby cells, the other prisoners looked on with interest.

"Tommy," said Langford, "I've got some good news for you. Jim Bandy is alive. Your bullet didn't kill him!"

Ben Sanders stood in stunned silence and watched joy spread over the faces of the two young people while Marshal Bart Langford explained the misunderstanding as to which Jim had died in the shooting.

While Tommy and Melinda clung to each other and wept for joy, Langford said, "Son, you'll still have to stand trial for shooting Jim Bandy, but actually it may work out for the best. This way, the townspeople will hear all the facts, and you will be cleared of any guilt in the robbery. Payton Roads's testimony, alone, should take care of that."

Tommy nodded tearfully, unable to speak.

"I'm going to testify that I fully believe you rode to the B-Bar-S for the purpose of turning yourself in. I will also tell the judge and jury how you risked your life to help subdue Turk Killam yesterday. I have absolutely no doubt that the jury will acquit you, especially with Ben Sanders giving testimony of your fine character and hard work at the ranch."

Langford's eyes found Sanders's.

"Oh . . . uh . . . yes, yes, of course," said the rancher, still somewhat stunned.

Smiling broadly, the marshal said, "It will all work out okay, Tommy. I'm sure of it. So if you decide to stay in these parts, you'll be able to walk down the streets of El Paso with your head up high."

"Oh, Tommy!" exclaimed Melinda. "I love you! Everything is going to be all right!"

Tommy breathed a shaky, "I love you, too, Melinda," and through the bars kissed her tenderly.

After a long pause, Ben Sanders hesitantly stepped close to the happy couple and said sheepishly, "Tommy, I owe you an apology. I've been wrong. I should have given you the benefit of the doubt in all this and stood beside you. Please forgive this old hardhead."

"It's all right, Mr. Sanders," Tommy replied softly. "You're just human like the rest of us."

"And Melinda," said Sanders, lower lip quivering, "I've been wrong in attempting to pick a mate for you. I can see how much you and Tommy love each other. Can you find it in your heart to forgive your old dad?"

The golden-haired young woman let go of Tommy and embraced her father. Kissing his cheek, she said, "All is forgiven."

Turning to young Taubert, the silver-haired rancher said, "Tommy, you know how pleased I've been with your work and the way you get along with the men. Well, I'm planning to retire within the next two or three years. Evelyn and I will be moving to El Paso. It sure would be great if I had a son-in-law who could take over the ranch."

Melinda's eyes were swimming.

Looking at his daughter, Ben Sanders grinned furtively and added, "That is, if Melinda is of a mind to say yes when you pop the question!"

Immediately, Tommy looked at Melinda. Reaching through the bars and taking both her hands in his own, he said, "This isn't the most ideal place to ask it, Melinda, but *will you marry me?*"

Eyes glistening with tears, lovely Melinda whispered, "Yes, Tommy, my love. I will marry you."

Jack Taubert could not recall how many times he had

fallen beneath the weight of his precious gold. But he staggered to his feet again. The cold night wind chilled the feverish sweat that poured from his weakening body, stamping haggard lines on his angular features. The strength was draining from his legs with every agonizing step.

Down he went again, pivoting as he fell, so that he landed on his back. In his delirium, the full moon blazed down at him like a ball of fire that lanced through his eyelids like red-hot irons. He rolled his head on the frigid sand like a sick man on a pillow. Mumbling to himself to get up, he strained against the ropes that held the heavy bags on his shoulders and once again stood upright.

As Jack stumbled forward across the cold, moonlit desert, his body burned with a fire that convinced him it was midday. He kept lifting his hand to ward off the oppressive rays of the moon. He yearned for water, and suddenly, more than a hundred yards ahead of him, he saw the edge of a huge lake, sparkling like sapphire in the moonlight. Its waters were cool and inviting.

Expending the last of his energy, he staggered forward like a drunken man, crying, "Water! I see you! Beautiful, beautiful water!"

When the thirst-crazed outlaw had covered the hundred yards, he found nothing but sand. His knees buckled, and he dropped to a kneeling position, swaying like a palm tree on a wind-whipped tropical island.

Jack reached up and tore at his shirt, ripping away the collar. His throat was on fire. His tongue cleaved to the roof of his mouth and was swelling. A wave of nausea swept over him, followed by a quick feverish chill.

"Gotta . . . gotta keep going," he gasped. "Can't stop now."

A faint shadow passed over him in the bright moonlight, followed by another and then another. He lifted his red eyes toward the purple sky but saw nothing.

Sheer grit put him on his feet again. He stumbled a few more steps. His breathing was labored, with the insides of his lungs as dry as the sand under his feet. The furnacelike fever seemed to ignite his brain.

Jack took two more steps, swayed heavily, and then took two more. For a brief moment, he hovered between heaven and earth, while the three broad-winged shadows passed over him again. Then he collapsed.

Lying on the sand, Jack struggled to rise, but the four bags were holding him down. From somewhere inside him, a whispering voice said, "Leave the gold! Leave the gold and go on!"

From his pit-dry mouth came a long, "No-o-o-o!"

Jack Taubert would never leave his gold. It was his god, and he would not be so profane as to abandon his god. He would die first.

In a sudden flash of clarity, he realized that was exactly what he was going to do: *die*. Turning on his belly, he puffed and grunted, tucking the priceless canvas bags close to his sides.

With shaky hands, he unbuttoned his shirt pocket, pulling out the wrinkled bank draft Tommy had given him. Fumbling in the pocket again, he said hoarsely, "They'll know. Yes, they will! They'll know that . . . that it ended right."

Producing a pencil stub, he gasped for breath around his swollen tongue and turned the back of the draft face up. Flattening it against the palm of his left hand, he scribbled the words, "DIED RICH!"

With a final dry wheeze, Jack Taubert laughed weakly. His face dropped into the sand, he puffed dust twice, and then he lay still. The cold desert breeze plucked at his long, stringy hair. His fingers clutched the note in a death grip.

The three huge vultures swooped lower this time and then touched ground a few feet away. The cool eye of the moon watched their shiny heads twist on raw, red necks while they waited to see if the fallen form would move again.

Lucy Daniels and Branson Howard were discussing

their marriage plans over the table at the Little Sombrero Café when Marshal Bart Langford returned. Sitting down, he called to the waitress for coffee and then turned his attention on the starry-eyed couple. They were holding hands across the corner of the table.

"Well," said Langford, "don't tell me you two are serious about each other."

Without pulling his gaze from Lucy's beautiful face, Branson said, "Serious as two broken legs, Marshal. Lucy is going to be Mrs. Branson Howard."

Langford guffawed and slapped his leg. "Well, if that don't beat all! Looks like there's gonna be wedding bells ringing twice in El Paso real soon!"

"Oh?" said Branson, turning to look at the lawman.

"Yep. Tommy Taubert and Ben Sanders's daughter are getting hitched, too."

"Then everything's going to be all right for the kid?"

"No doubt about it." The marshal grinned.

"That's wonderful," said Lucy. "I'm glad."

"Now, about the other Taubert," said Langford seriously, "I figure with some night riding, we can catch him within a couple of days. Taubert is hauling a lot of dead weight. What say we leave after I take Tommy to the judge?"

"Forget it," the Texas Ranger said blandly. "I've already wired the Arizona authorities to pick up Jack in Tucson. I've got to be on the stage to Austin tomorrow. Have to get that gold delivered so I can hurry back and get married."

Slack jawed and flustered, Langford gruffed, "What on earth are you talking about?"

Grinning slyly, Branson said, "Finish your coffee, and I'll show you something."

Eyeing him with mild suspicion, Lucy said, "Branson Howard, what have you done?"

"You will see, my sweet," chuckled the Ranger.

Five minutes later, Lucy and the two lawmen entered the Lone Star Stagecoach Company barn. The bright red Concord coach stood in the middle of the straw-covered floor. Under watchful eyes, Branson went to the toolbox in the boot and pulled out a crowbar. Opening the door of the Concord, he inserted the narrow tip of the bar under one of the floorboards and jimmied it loose.

With his fingers, Branson raised the board, exposing neatly packed canvas bags lying on a false floor.

Langford's eyes bulged. "The gold!" he gasped.

Lucy was speechless.

Branson dropped the board into place and tapped it tight with the rounded end of the crowbar. While Lucy smiled with amusement, he explained that after arriving from Austin on the last run, Sam Neff and Ray Ringdon had followed his directions and built in the false floor. Henry Yates did not know of Branson's plan, but thought that Neff and Ringdon were making normal repairs on the stagecoach inside the barn.

Lifting his hat and scratching his head, the marshal asked, "Well, when did you move the gold from the bank vault to the coach?"

"I didn't. The gold was never in the bank."

"Aw, come on, Branson," Langford said in disbelief. "How could that be?"

"My superiors in Austin gave me full rein to do whatever I had to in order to deliver the gold safely," replied Branson. "At the very beginning, I directed the three Pinkerton men to bring the gold right here into the barn when they brought it from New Mexico."

Smiling at Langford's look of shock, the Ranger continued, "There's a hole over there in the corner under that grain barrel. It's covered with boards that are camouflaged by a layer of dirt and straw. The Pinkerton men dug the hole and hid the gold in there."

Langford broke into a hearty laugh, holding his ample belly. "Branson," he roared, "I've got to hand it to you! Boy, did you ever put one over on Turk Killam . . . *and* Jack Taubert!"

Brow furrowed, Lucy said to the man she loved, "But what is Jack Taubert carrying?"

Chuckling, Branson toyed with his mustache. "Nothing but gold-colored iron pyrite."

"*Fool's gold!*" exclaimed the marshal, still laughing.

"Right!" Branson grinned. "I knew if somebody did hit the bank for the gold, they would be in too much of a hurry to take the time to study it close."

It was Lucy's turn to laugh. "And Jack Taubert thinks he's rich!"

"That's right," said Branson, folding the captivating woman into his arms. "But I'm the one who's rich. I have you!"